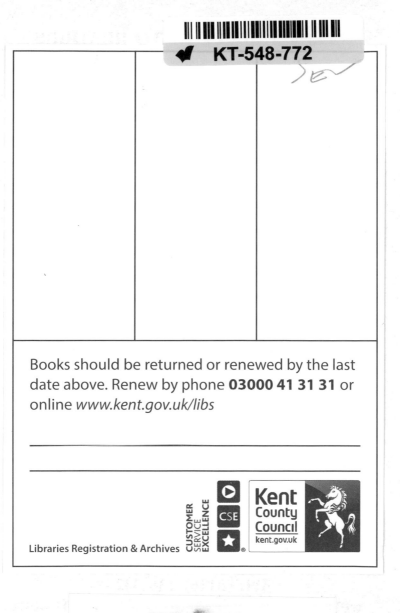

Books should be returned or renewed by the last date above. Renew by phone **03000 41 31 31** or online *www.kent.gov.uk/libs*

Libraries Registration & Archives

CUSTOMER SERVICE EXCELLENCE

CSE

Kent County Council
kent.gov.uk

MISSION: TANK WAR

1960s: A small, oil-rich Arab nation is about to lose its status as a protectorate of Britain, and waiting in the wings to invade is a superior enemy force led by Soviet tanks. On a mission to stop them is debonair agent Peter Carthage and the men from War (Weapons Analysis and Research), Inc., a company with an ultra-scientific approach to warfare. How many men from War, Inc. does it take to stop an army of tanks? Six — plus one beautiful, plucky young British woman determined to rescue a kidnapped brother.

MICHAEL KURLAND

MISSION:
TANK WAR

Complete and Unabridged

LINFORD
Leicester

First published in Great Britain

First Linford Edition
published 2016

A catalogue record for this book is available
from the British Library.

ISBN 978–1–4448–2987–7

Published by
F. A. Thorpe (Publishing)
Anstey, Leicestershire

Set by Words & Graphics Ltd.
Anstey, Leicestershire
Printed and bound in Great Britain by
T. J. International Ltd., Padstow, Cornwall

This book is printed on acid-free paper

To E. A. Jones
in acknowledgment of technical assistance for which I am very grateful,
and with the deepest admiration

1

It could have been a scene from a Grade C movie. A company of soldiers crouched around the wall circling a pumping station were valiantly defending it against native tribesmen. The tribesmen, their white robes flapping as they rode around the station, screamed ancient curses in Arabic. Their long Craig rifles cracked red flame, and the defenders' sub-machine guns stuttered white streams of tracer slugs into the night. As in the movies, an occasional man would crumple behind the wall or slide off his horse, eyes wide and hands at his chest as a widening splotch of red stained his tunic.

But the blood was real. The battle had gone on for half an hour, with neither side gaining an advantage, when an anachronism appeared. A high-winged monoplane flew into sight and began making purposeful circles over the battle area. This observer took neither side, and the combatants, from lack of choice, ignored the plane. Over the droning sound of the engine and the sharp bursts of gunfire could be heard the clacking of a heavy camera shutter within the plane, if anyone below paused long enough to listen for it.

In director's-chair position on a sand dune overlooking the action, a tall man in the garb of a desert chieftain sat astride a milk-white Arabian stallion and stared impassively at the scene below. Emotion crossed his face only twice: one brief moment of savage joy when the tribesmen succeeded in blowing up a pipeline where it entered the station, and again a trace of bewilderment when the plane appeared.

At an almost imperceptible hand signal from the chieftain, the tribesmen left the attack and gathered in a group just out of range of the wall. Several figures dropped and remained flat on the sand, while the group rode a quarter of the way around the circle to draw the defenders' attention. The figures then stealthily crawled back to the attack line to retrieve the wounded and dead. Easily spotted from above, the crawling figures were almost invisible to the soldiers crouched low behind the wall.

Motionless and silent except for the heavy breathing of their horses, the tribesmen sat facing the wall. Now the pulsing drone of the overhead airplane was the loudest sound on the desert, and some of the men below did hear a strange clacking noise and wonder at it. One of the riders left the group and guided his horse up the loose sand of the tall dune until he was beside his chief. 'Thy servant, Mondar,' he intoned.

'I rule among equals, ben Sinna.' The tall man continued staring across the sand, and he spoke softly, but his voice carried clearly across the desert.

There was a silence lasting several minutes; then the tall man turned his head to look at his companion. 'The station does not fall, ben Sinna.'

Ben Sinna inclined his head briefly. 'True, Mondar. The exchange of death has been just about equal, perhaps just slightly more of them than us. We are following your plan,' ben Sinna said, keeping his voice carefully noncommittal. 'We stay at a precise distance from the station, keep in motion, and fire only at targets or at the flashes from their guns.'

Mondar looked sharply at his lieutenant. 'You disapprove?'

'My chief,' ben Sinna said, keeping his voice low and speaking earnestly, 'for years — for generations — el Quarat, the people whose title you bear as Sherif el Quarat, our hereditary leader, first among equals, have been the most feared tribe in the desert. We are fighters: it is our birth; it is our learning; it is our creed. We shall do battle until the egg of the world cracks open, and until this time your house will lead us. It isn't my place to approve your decisions.'

'But if it were,' Mondar asked dryly, 'is it safe to say that you wouldn't approve?'

'Your father,' ben Sinna said, stroking his slight beard and managing to sound as if he were conveying ancient wisdom, 'and your grandfather led us in many battles. Our tribe, alone and with others, has taken many strong points. And today thirty men are holding off our two hundred. The method of fighting used by your grandfather worked well for him and his son. When taking a fortified point,' he said, enumerating on his long fingers, 'first surround it from high points in the dunes, allowing no one in or out. Then gradually work closer and tighten the ring, taking a period of days if you must. The longer you wait the less food and water will remain in the fort.' Ben Sinna looked as though he were reliving old experiences as he spoke. 'If you can, starve them out. Have your sharpshooters fire at anyone foolish enough to show his head. Wear them down through fatigue, thirst and fear. Then, when they are no longer able to put up an organized resistance, the attack! A sudden surprise charge by all our horsemen, sweeping aside their poor defense and bearing us right inside the fort. One moment of final victory and glory.' He brought his right hand down with a slapping sound that startled his horse.

'My grandfather fought with a flintlock rifle,' Mondar reminded his captain, 'and his grandfather carried a spear. Times

5

change, and we must change along with them. We cannot lie on the dunes and keep them surrounded for many days, because they have radio transmitters, and rescue will arrive with the sun. We cannot charge the station directly, because although we outnumber them by seven men to one, they're carrying automatic weapons — machine guns — that give one of their men fighting equality with ten of ours at close range.'

'So instead,' ben Sinna said, 'we ride around their station many times, yelling and tiring our horses. I fail to see the logic of your solution.'

'When you talk to me, ben Sinna, you don't seem to be able to decide whether you're addressing your leader, which I am, or your pupil, which I have been most of my life. Your tone fights between respect and scolding.'

Ben Sinna thought about this for a moment. 'True,' he finally acknowledged, staring up at the plane, which was making a low pass over the waiting horsemen.

'Ignore that,' Mondar said.

Ben Sinna sighed. 'We are, I suppose,

to go back to the circling, yelling and shooting now that the horses are to some degree rested.'

'Patience for a while,' Mondar suggested. 'This has served its purpose.'

'It has?'

'Truly. In an hour we have done what took my grandfather two or three days of biding behind sand dunes. By circling just out of range of the machine guns, and sharpshooting with our more accurate rifles, we have made them nervous, afraid and less able to resist.'

'We have?'

'Let's hope so. It is now time for the next step.'

'Ah,' ben Sinna agreed, none the wiser, 'the next step.'

'The siege train, the battering rams, the, ah, heavy artillery. Go back to the men and prepare them to attack. I am about to destroy the enemy's will to resist — along with just about everything else inside those walls.'

Thus dismissed, ben Sinna silently wheeled his horse and rode back to the waiting men, leaving his chief staring impassively at something off in the distance.

As ben Sinna rode off, Mondar pulled a long silver whistle from his robe and blew two shrill blasts on it. The sound reverberated over the dunes.

★   ★   ★

Inside the station a short, stocky lieutenant crouched against the wall and peered out at the horsemen through a large pair of binoculars. He watched while one of the riders left the main group and joined the leader on a hill carefully out of rifle shot.

'I say, what are those bloody maniacs doing now?'

The lieutenant turned. A tall, thin young man in the approved desert dress of the Anglo-Jeppet Oil Company — short-sleeved khaki shirt, khaki Bermuda shorts, khaki knee socks and light brown desert boots — stood next to him and nervously patted a very sparse blond mustache.

'A combination of conference and tea-time, I imagine,' the lieutenant suggested.

8

'Please keep your head down. You're making it too easy for them.'

The young man dropped to a squatting position. 'It's all right for you,' he complained, 'but I didn't come out here to get scalped by a bunch of savages. You're paid for this sort of thing. I'm supposed to be an oil consultant.'

'Think of it as the will of Allah, Mister Quinline. Besides, these particular savages don't scalp: their established custom is to cut throats.' The lieutenant made an illustrative gesture with his hand.

Quinline shuddered. 'That's all very nice, but . . . ' He paused as the lieutenant readjusted the binoculars and stared into them. 'What's happening now?'

'The conference seems to be over. The conferee is rejoining the group. Time for us to look alive again.' The lieutenant called a runner over to him. 'Wake up the men and tell them that things are about to get hot again.'

'Yes, sir.' The runner started on a circuit of the wall.

The lieutenant picked up his Sten gun and checked it. 'We've got enough ammunition left for about another half hour of this nonsense,' he told Quinline.

'That doesn't really sound very re-assuring, Lieutenant Akrat. What about reinforcements?'

'I had Port Hornblower on the radio about ten minutes ago. A relief column is on the way now, but it can't get here for at least two hours. They wish us luck.'

'British?' Quinline asked.

'The Royal Army of Jeppet, like myself,' Lieutenant Akrat said. 'It's a matter of jurisdiction.'

'I see,' said Quinline, who didn't. 'What about that damned plane?' He pointed to make it clear which plane he was referring to.

'I told them about it. They assured me that it isn't one of ours, and it's very doubtful that it belongs to our friends out there. They admit to being puzzled and promise to look into it the first chance they get.'

'Splendid,' the young man said bitterly. 'I don't suppose . . . ' The sharp, shrill blast of a whistle sounded twice from the top of the dunes and echoed off the buildings behind them.

'What was that?' Quinline demanded, the strain showing in his voice.

'I'm not sure,' Lieutenant Akrat said, laying his Sten gun on the wall and sighting carefully along the top of it. 'I'd have thought it was the signal to attack, but they don't seem to be attacking. Whatever it means, I don't suppose it's anything we'll like very much. If you want to help, you could pick up a spare gun and find yourself a vacant spot along the wall.'

'As I told you before, Lieutenant,' Quinline said stiffly, 'the Anglo-Jeppet Oil Company doesn't permit its employees to engage in any sort of armed activity. That's to be left to the local police and military.'

'They're not going to ask, you know,' the lieutenant said.

'What's that?'

'Our friends outside. They're not going to ask about your company's regulations. If, by some miracle, you're still alive when they overrun the station, they'll slit your throat — and then you won't be. At least keep out of the way; stay here and keep down.'

Quinline sat on the hard-packed sand with his back to the wall. 'I suppose you think I'm a coward,' he said. Lieutenant Akrat shrugged and said nothing. 'It's not that,' Quinline told him. 'When I took this job, I did so on the assurance that there'd be no fighting involved — I know how oil companies seem to end up in the middle of battles. You see, I'm a pacifist. I believe in the principles of nonviolence.'

Something moved in the distance, but it was too far away to tell what it was yet, and there wasn't anything the lieutenant could do about it anyway. Quinline seemed to want to talk, so Akrat humored him. 'There are many people who don't believe in violence,' he said.

'That's passive,' Quinline explained, 'not believing in something. What I mean is an active belief in nonviolence. Standing up for what you feel is right, even when the other fellow blacks your eye for it, but not striking back. The Christian principle of turning the other cheek.'

'I'm a follower of Islam, Mister

Quinline. Mohammed teaches one to live by the sword.'

'Violence is wrong,' Quinline insisted. 'Morally wrong. It's time the human race outgrew it.'

'It's time for a lot of things that haven't happened yet,' Akrat said.

The distant object had moved closer, and Akrat could now make it out. It was a single heavily loaded camel, led by three natives. Akrat picked up his binoculars for a closer look. On the back of the camel, weaving about in time with the beast's ponderous walk, was a long tube.

Akrat gave a low whistle and gestured with his free hand. The runner returned, keeping his head carefully below the top of the wall. 'Tell our sharpshooter on the roof to see if he can pot that animal before it gets any closer,' Akrat said. The soldier nodded and raced away, headed for one of the buildings.

Quinline took the binoculars and peered through them. 'What's that thing on the camel's back?' he asked.

'I was wondering about that myself. About the only thing I can think of that

13

would make sense is a recoilless rifle.'

'A rifle?'

'A recoilless rifle. Think of it as an easily portable cannon.'

The beast stopped, and flame suddenly shot out of both ends of the long tube. A thin line of fire arched over the station, accompanied by a loud roaring noise.

'That's what it is,' Akrat commented, as the sound of an explosion came from close behind them. 'But they seem to be aiming high.'

'The camel lurched,' said Quinline, who still had the binoculars.

'I shouldn't wonder. A camel isn't the most stable firing platform in the world. Besides, the sound of the shot probably scared the poor beast half to death.'

The tube flamed again. This time the shot plowed a furrow in the sand before exploding some ten yards in front of the wall.

'Short,' the lieutenant said.

There was a sharp cracking sound over their heads, and Quinline instinctively dropped.

'That's our sharpshooter,' Akrat said.

'It's extreme range for him, pure luck if he hits anything.'

'Oh, sorry,' Quinline said, sitting up and dusting himself off.

'There's no shame in ducking when there are bullets flying,' the lieutenant said. He took the binoculars from Quinline and resumed his watch. 'Only a fool or a fatalist is unafraid when facing a loaded gun.'

'Which are you?' Quinline asked bitterly, and without thinking.

'I'm afraid,' Lieutenant Akrat admitted softly. 'The mark of a man is that he does what he must despite fear, not without it.'

Quinline thought about it for a few seconds. 'That's true,' he said. 'They're taking the rifle off the camel's back,' Akrat said. 'We have a minute or so before they start up again, although I'm afraid this time their aim will be better.' He put down the binoculars.

'What's going to happen?' Quinline asked. 'I mean, to us?'

'We'll either hold out for two hours until the reinforcements get here, or we won't.'

'And if we don't?'

'Then we'll have the chance to discover which of our religions has the true picture of heaven.'

'I see,' Quinline told him. 'Can we hold out?'

'I doubt it,' Lieutenant Akrat told him. 'They'll batter down this wall with that gun and then come charging in. We'll retreat to the buildings for a last-ditch fight. One by one they'll take the buildings. Then they'll go around and slit the throat of anyone not already dead. They'll do their best to destroy the buildings; if they have any dynamite, they'll blow them up. Then they'll gather up their dead and wounded and ride home singing.'

'Why?' Quinline demanded. He stood up and stared blindly off across the sand. 'Why do they do this? Why do they hate us so?'

Lieutenant Akrat pulled him down. 'They don't hate you, Mister Quinline. This station represents change. For many hundreds of years the only changes have been bad.'

'You know a lot about them,' Quinline said.

'They're my people,' Lieutenant Akrat answered without expression.

'Your people?'

'In truth. I was born into that tribe.'

The recoilless rifle fired. This time the explosion was inside the wall. 'They're getting the range,' Akrat commented.

The next shot hit the wall, gouging out a small section and sending chips of cement flying. After that the rounds fell about one every twenty seconds, either on the wall or inside the station. Most were directed toward one small part of the wall, slowly reducing it to rubble. The horsemen were firing their rifles at the station now, and the combined noise was deafening.

'Why don't your men fire back?' Quinline demanded, the edge of hysteria in his voice.

Akrat looked at him with a peculiar expression. 'I'm prepared to respect your nonviolent beliefs, Mister Quinline, but you must be consistent.'

'Consistent?' Quinline shuddered. 'It's

hard to be consistent when you're in a state of panic. I never even liked the sound of target shooting at an amusement park. The only thing stopping me from getting up and running is that there's no place to run.'

'That's the effect they're trying to create. My men aren't firing back because there's no target within range, and they have orders not to waste their ammunition. There'll be plenty of shooting in a few minutes; that hole looks big enough for our friends to start thinking about charging through it.'

Akrat yelled for the runner and gave orders for most of the men on the far side of the wall to be brought around and stationed in the building facing the newly blasted hole.

The explosions were mostly coming from inside the station now. Dirt, sand, rock and chips of concrete formed a haze over the area and splattered to the ground like an irregular rainfall. The thick, acrid smog burned the lungs and eyes of the defenders.

The silver whistle sounded over the

firing, stopping the guns abruptly, and for a long moment the desert was silent. Then, oddly muted by the sand, the hoofbeats of many horses broke the quiet as el Quarat rode to the attack.

When the first line of tribesmen reached the wall, they let out a long, keening scream, which was picked up by the men behind them. A sub-machine gun chattered in reply to the scream, and one of the lead horses fell, throwing its rider. More sub-machine guns sounded, and the sharp crack of rifles answered as the riders galloped through the breach and into the station.

It was almost an hour before the desert was again silent.

2

The city of Ante, capital of the Sheikdom of Jeppet, is as old as human history. As far back as records go, on paper, papyrus and clay tablets, there has been some sort of settlement on this fertile strip between the great desert and the Persian Gulf. For as deep as archeologists care to dig, there is some sign of human habitation.

On the Gulf is the port, a whitewashed oval of former glories. In the port, thrust out from the oval like a middle finger, lay the Sheik's Dock, a long, stone pier built centuries ago by the rulers of Jeppet. From its sides triremes once went out to protect the wealth of ancient Akr, its pearl fishers, and, legend has it, to stop an occasional passing merchant ship and see whether it held anything that might be of interest to the Sheik.

Today the port is the point of departure for Jeppet's newly found oil wealth and is busier than it ever was. The Sheik's Dock, closed off by customs barriers, holds the incoming symbols of this wealth. Haphazardly stacked crates of air conditioners, adding machines, disassembled school desks, textbooks, shoes, cosmetics and heavy machinery cluttered the stone pier.

It was eight-fifteen in the morning, and Peter Carthage, head of the Weapons Analysis and Research, Inc. mission to Jeppet, was standing outside the customs shed, looking through the fence at the pile of crates. A taxi pulled up, and its passenger got out and strode over to Peter.

'Welcome, Tony,' Peter said, sticking out his hand.

Tony Ryan grabbed the hand and shook it briefly. 'Right,' he said, 'hospitality of the Mystic East and all that stuff. What am I doing here?'

'I sent for you,' Peter told him.

'I figured that, pal,' Tony said. 'Only my old buddy Carthage would call me away from a well-deserved month's vacation in Stockholm after the first week is barely up. It had the earmarks of Carthage consideration all over it. I repeat, what am I doing here?'

'Well,' Peter said, 'I tried to set up this mission without you, but nobody has insulted me for the past week. I felt that something was missing. I'm putting you in charge of the Plans and Strategy section of the mission.'

Tony tried to set his youthful face in a serious expression. 'Bad?' he asked.

'Bad,' Peter agreed.

'Twenty pasti,' the cabdriver said, sticking his head out of the window of the ancient Packard.

'What's that?' Tony asked.

'You owe me twenty pasti. Plus tip,' the cabdriver added thoughtfully.

'Look, hang on a second,' Tony told the cabdriver.

'How much,' he asked Peter confidentially, 'is a pasti?'

'It's a passit,' Peter told him. 'Pasti is the plural.'

'Great,' Tony said. 'What's it worth?'

'A passit is just about a quarter. Twenty pasti is about five bucks.'

'I'm being took,' Tony decided.

'You coming from the hotel?' Peter asked.

'What hotel? I got your message at the airport to meet you here, wherever this is, at eight o'clock, and here I am. Wherever.'

'Twenty pasti,' the cabdriver interjected.

'Where are your bags?'

'In the cab. Will our friend take anything but pasti? I've got Swedish and American money, but precious few pasti.'

'I'll take care of it,' Peter said. He went over to the cab and had a short, animated conversation with the driver. A few pieces of bright red paper changed hands, and the driver engaged the car's rasping gears and drove away in a cloud of oil.

'Where's he going with my irreplaceable luggage?' Tony asked. 'Am I going to have to buy them back at some local bazaar?'

'I had a hard time convincing him to handle such beat-up-looking bags,' Peter said, 'but he finally agreed to take them to the hotel and sneak them up the back way.'

'Good of him,' Tony said. 'Now that you've pulled me four thousand miles to swipe my luggage, tell me what's happening.'

'Fair enough,' Peter said. 'This is the customs office for the Sheik's Dock, which is that stone causeway past the building. We're waiting for the office to open so we can get in and inspect some goods.'

'When does it open?' Tony asked.

'The sign says it opened twenty minutes ago,' Peter said, 'only there's no one here yet. I'm sorry to have rushed you. Have you had any sleep?'

'Not in weeks,' Tony said. 'Drone some soporific facts into my ear while we're waiting, and we'll find out if sleep learning really works.' He settled himself comfortably against the wooden fence and closed his eyes.

Peter sat down on a convenient crate and tried to decide where to begin. For him it had begun four days before in War, Inc.'s headquarters in New Jersey. Dr. Steadman, the almost mythical 'Old Man,' former head of Special Intelligence Group during World War Two, and founder of War, Inc., had called Peter into his office.

'What do you know about Arabs?' he

had asked Peter without waiting for him to sit down.

'The usual things,' Peter had answered, lowering himself into the soft leather chair opposite the desk. 'White horses, scimitars, oasis with date palms and beautiful houris, endless deserts, and so on.'

'You read a book,' Steadman said accusingly.

'Saw a movie,' Peter admitted.

'Well, forget it,' Steadman said. 'I'm sending you to Jeppet.'

'The place with all the oil?' Peter asked.

'That's it,' Steadman agreed. 'We're setting up a mission in Jeppet, and you're it.'

★ ★ ★

Weapons Analysis and Research, Inc., Dr. Steadman's creation, supplied advice and training to the military establishments of small independent countries. Acting under the theory that until men are capable of living in peace, a good defense is the best assurance against war, these modern mercenaries, with the paradoxical title of War,

Inc., were dedicated to keeping the peace. A small country threatened by external aggression or internal subversion might need help in handling the situation. Applying to one of the big powers for aid could be considered to have political overtones. The smaller 'powers' might be willing to help, but the strings attached to the offer were usually thick and long. So free enterprise took a hand. War, Inc. expected to be paid for its services, but asked nothing more. This lack of strings, as Dr. Steadman had foreseen, proved attractive to many small countries with a military problem.

Before accepting any government as a client, Dr. Steadman and his staff made as sure as possible that the country's intentions were purely defensive; one wrong guess in that regard and the tacit support that he received from the nations within whose borders War, Inc. operated or had offices would be quickly withdrawn. So far Steadman had managed to guess right.

3

'What do you know about Jeppet?' Peter asked Tony.

'I didn't even know the place existed before I got here,' Tony said without opening his eyes, 'but now you might say I'm an expert. I've been here a whole half hour.'

'I'll start from the beginning,' Peter told him. 'I've been here three days now, so I should be able to answer your questions.'

'Three days,' Tony agreed, 'is half a lifetime.'

'Jeppet is a Sheikdom which was set up as a British protectorate under a League of Nations mandate after World War One. Its traditional industries are pearl fishing and goat raising, neither one of which was a source of wealth.'

'Pearls,' Tony stated from behind closed eyes, 'are expensive.'

'True,' Peter said, 'but they're also hard

to come by. If you had any idea of how many oysters you have to examine to find one pearl, you'd take up goat raising.'

'I thought they seeded oysters to make them produce pearls.'

'They do now, but that's a recent technique. Anyway, the good citizens of Jeppet have something better now. Under your feet right at this moment is an estimated one-seventh of the world's oil reserve.'

Tony opened his eyes and looked down. 'It looks like sand,' he said.

'You're tired,' Peter told him. 'Close your eyes. To continue, since the discovery of oil here in nineteen forty-seven, the citizens of Jeppet have acquired what may be described as moderate wealth. The wells are actually owned by the Sheik of Jeppet, but he has distributed freely among his subjects the royalty paid him by the Anglo-Jeppet Oil Company. This largesse has been mostly in the form of new schools and hospitals. There is now a large middle class, and no poor. All kinds of new government projects provide work for the people and pay well. Education, from kindergarten through the new

University of Akr, is free for any citizen.

'That's quoted, as closely as I can remember, out of the government's information folder. The most prevalent sign of new wealth that I can find is a universal ownership of air conditioners. A lot of the homes that don't have electricity yet have air conditioners already installed, awaiting the great day. Within the next two years, the government claims, every home in the state will be electrified.'

'Sounds like a desert paradise,' Tony commented. 'What do they need us for?'

'The land of Nod,' Peter said, 'which the Bible tells us is somewhere east of Eden, is trying to spread west.'

'I'll allow you to explain that statement,' Tony said.

'Fair enough. Have you ever heard of the Desert Legion?'

'I get a picture,' Tony said, holding one hand to his forehead. 'Let me concentrate. I see a group of horsemen with flowing white burnooses — or is it burnii? In the lead I see Lawrence of Arabia riding a motorcycle and waving a long sword. It's a silent movie with a honky-tonk piano accompaniment.'

'It's a good image,' Peter said, 'but the truth is a bit more serious. The Desert Legion is the romantic name of a group of cutthroats headed by an ex-Nazi general named Brontke.'

Tony opened his eyes. 'That's right,' he said, 'I remember now. It's a sort of Arab Foreign Legion. The men are from half the jails in the world and are wanted in the other half. They're as good as stateless, because if one of them goes to the customs window of any border he'll be thrown in jail to wait for extradition by whichever country wants him most. The officers are renegades from most of the unsuccessful mutinies and revolutions of the past twenty years. They've shown up all over the Near East practicing aggression, revolution and subversion. They're equipped with some of the most modern weapons around and seem never to lack for money. The big mystery is who pays them. It's believed to be Egypt, since they seem usually to be furthering Nasser's foreign policy, but there's no proof. They were the ones involved in the invasion of

Kuthemat when the King was murdered. They had to be driven off with British troops.'

'That's them,' Peter said. 'Now you've got it.'

A high whining sound coming from the far end of the street fronting the pier caused them both to look up. Slowly and majestically a large square black box with windows was rounding the corner. It whined up the street toward them on silent hard rubber tires and stopped in front of them.

'Migod,' Tony breathed, 'what the hell is that doing here?'

'What the hell is it?' Peter asked.

'An early Cleveland Electric,' Tony said. 'Which is sort of redundant; there aren't any late ones. This one must be about nineteen eleven.'

The window rolled down, and a gentleman with a short, neat spade beard and a blue visored cap stuck his head out. 'Nineteen ought nine,' he corrected.

'Sorry about that,' Tony said. 'It's a beautiful thing nonetheless.'

'I agree, of course,' the gentleman said.

He surveyed Peter and Tony closely, peering up and down through the window, and then rolled up the window and climbed out of the car. 'You must be Colonels Carthage and Ryan.'

'Well,' Tony said, 'if I must.'

'Of course you are,' the man insisted. 'You fit the description.' He pulled a paper from the tunic pocket of his blue uniform, which was plastered with gold braid at all the appropriate — and several unusual — places. 'Colonel Carthage,' he read from the paper, 'above average height, brown eyes, blond hair, trim build; Colonel Ryan, medium height, black thick hair — probably uncombed, dark eyes, bowlegged and with a pronounced squint. You don't,' he said to Tony accusingly, 'seem to be bowlegged or have a squint.'

'You're an excessively literal man,' Tony said. He glared at Peter. 'I can guess who wrote those descriptions.'

'It seemed a good idea at the time,' Peter said.

'Also, neither of you is in uniform,' the man said. 'Perhaps I should ask you for identification, just as a matter of form.'

'The colonelcy is an equivalent rank,' Peter explained, pulling out his passport. 'We're here as advisers to the Army.'

'So I understand,' the man said. He took the two passports and examined them closely.

'You must be the customs agent we were to meet here,' Peter said.

'I,' the man announced, 'am General Huit, chief of the Sheik's Customs Force.'

'My pleasure, General,' Peter said, extending his hand.

The customs general shook it in one brief up-and-down motion and handed the passports back. 'You're a bit early,' he said, 'but come along inside.'

'Early?' Peter asked. 'I thought you opened at eight o'clock.'

'Ah!' General Huit said. 'An honest mistake. You have misread the sign, which is meant to indicate that this office opens at the first high tide of the day, but in no case earlier than eight o'clock.' He fitted a large ornate key into the padlock on the wooden door.

'Naturally,' Peter said, 'a misunderstanding.'

The sign, lettered neatly on the side of the door, still said 'OPEN 800 TO 1700 HOURS' in both English and Arabic.

'The high tide today being at eight forty-seven, I am actually a bit early,' General Huit said, 'but I'm a conscientious worker.' He ushered them into the small office. 'The freighter *Moon of Irriwadi*, which holds the cargo you are awaiting, should be tying up at the dock any time now. One would presume that, being deck cargo, yours would be the first unloaded. Make yourselves comfortable. I must go open the gates for the dockworkers.' He waved them to a wooden bench and scurried out a side door.

'Make yourself,' Peter snorted, 'comfortable!' He sat down on the eight-inch-wide strip of board and leaned back against the slat wall.

Tony sat beside him. 'Finish your explanation.'

'What don't you know?'

'Well, for example, what has the Desert Legion got to do with us?'

'They're why we're here,' Peter explained. 'In just about six weeks Jeppet loses its

34

status as a protectorate of Britain and becomes an independent country. It was supposed to take several years, but pressure in the United Nations made Britain agree to rush it. It's a condition that the people of Jeppet, or, at any rate, those that know what's going on, aren't in favor of. The day that Jeppet becomes an independent country, Britain can no longer intervene in the country's problems. And it looks as if on that day, or shortly after, Jeppet is going to have a big problem. The Desert Legion is massed somewhere on the border, ready to march in.'

'I see,' Tony said, 'to be stopped by the Army of Jeppet, which consists of?'

'Which is made up of two troops of very showy cavalry at the present time. There are also three battalions of British troops here, but of course, the day after independence is declared they won't be here anymore. The Sheik of Jeppet would like them to stay, but Her Majesty's Government can't see its way clear to do that. It would be denounced as colonialism by all those who aren't going to get murdered when the Desert Legion comes riding in. Latest reports indicate that the legion will be riding in tanks.'

'Tanks?'

'Right. That's why I sent for you; I understand you're something of an expert on the beasties.'

'I drove one once,' Tony admitted.

'During the Korean War,' Peter said. 'You commanded a company of Shermans.'

'So did a lot of other people,' Tony said.

'You got a Silver Star,' Peter continued.

'They were being handed out like candy,' Tony said. 'As a matter of fact, if I remember correctly, candy was quite a bit harder to get. Except for that GI chocolate.'

'You then wrote a book on tank tactics that's in use now by three armies.'

Tony admitted this.

The desk phone rang and General Huit came racing inside to answer it. He said 'Yes, sir' several times, and then called to Peter, 'It's for you.'

Peter got up from the uncomfortable wooden bench and went to the desk. 'Hello?'

'Colonel Carthage?' the tinny voice on the phone asked.

'Speaking.'

'This is Sadi ben Dulli. I just wanted to make sure you were still there. I'll be coming to pick you up in a few minutes, if you don't mind; there's something I'd like to show you.'

'That's fine,' Peter said. 'I'll be expecting you.'

'Very good,' ben Dulli said, and hung up.

'Who was that?' Tony asked.

'The defense minister,' Peter said, 'who also happens to be the Sheik's brother.'

'Ah,' Tony said. 'I was wondering why the general looked so impressed.'

'Gentlemen,' General Huit called from the far door, 'if you would come out on the pier with me, this way please, your cargo is being downloaded now.'

'What is our cargo?' Tony whispered to Peter as they made their way out to the dock.

'You'll see in a second,' Peter said. 'You can't miss it.'

The *Moon of Irriwadi*, a freighter of

ancient and indeterminate lineage, was tied up at the far end of the pier. Three large shrouded forms were on its deck. As they walked closer to the ship, the canvas shrouds were taken off the objects, and the tackle of the ship's hoists was fastened around the forward bulk.

'I should have guessed,' Tony said. 'Tanks.'

The first one was lifted high off the deck of the ship, swung slowly and gently over the side and lowered to the dock in one smooth motion.

'Whoever's handling that ship's crane is a real pro,' Peter said approvingly.

'That tank looks a lot like a Sherman,' Tony said.

'Right,' Peter agreed.

'It must be an antique,' Tony said. 'I thought they stopped making them in forty-three. The ones we used in Korea were already ancient.'

'It's the best we could do on short notice,' Peter said. 'We'll have more modern ones on order as soon as possible, but they'll take a while to get here. We have to prepare for a possible tank invasion in six weeks to two months. We'll take what we can get.'

'Good enough,' Tony agreed. 'I hope they're in some kind of running order. We're going to have a hell of a time getting parts.'

4

In the desert somewhere southwest of the border of Jeppet, on that large area of sand waste that no country felt obliged to claim formally or police, squatted a large body of tanks, half-tracks, tents, horses, camels and men. It collectively called itself the Desert Legion, and admitted to no allegiance except expediency. In a large battle-green tent to one side of the area, General Brontke, commanding officer of the Desert Legion, met with his aides.

At the center of the tent was a large low table surrounded by steel folding chairs. The table had a four-inch lip around its edge and was filled with sand. On the sand, which had been shaped to model the dunes and depressions of desert terrain, miniature tanks, command cars and half-tracks faced each other in mock battle.

General Brontke, a tall man with a

large hooked nose and a small, precisely clipped mustache, stood at the foot of the display. Except for small changes in insignia, his uniform, like those of his aides, was a faithful copy of the garb of Hitler's Wehrmacht. Brontke bent over the board. 'Here, here and here,' he said, using his swagger stick as a pointer to indicate three dots on the miniature dunes. An aide carefully moved three columns of toy tanks to the positions indicated.

Brontke straightened up and ran a hand through his carefully combed gray hair. He looked satisfied. 'Well?' he asked the man standing opposite him.

Colonel Bahar, Brontke's second-in-command, a short, thick, black-haired man whose uniforms always looked two sizes too tight, paused and bit his lip. He looked as worried as Brontke looked confident.

'Come on, come on,' Brontke said, 'your enemy isn't going to give you time to think.'

'Yes, of course,' Bahar muttered. 'Right. Yes.'

'Well?' Brontke demanded.

'Straight in,' said Bahar uncertainly.

'Is that a statement or a question?' Brontke asked scornfully.

'Straight in,' Bahar declared; 'both columns.' He clenched his hands together while the aide moved the models, and then, realizing what he was doing, locked his hands carefully behind him.

'Bah!' Brontke snorted. 'Anti-tank guns pulled up to here,' he said, drawing the point of his swagger stick across a dune, 'along this line. Panzers forward and disperse in firing order. Engage the enemy!' He slapped the swagger stick against his left palm while his orders were carried out.

'Two files, right and left,' Bahar said, and his models were advanced to meet the attack. 'Engage and commence firing,' he said, sounding resigned to his fate,

'Tigers forward!' Brontke commanded. From over a dune to the left, four tank models were pushed forward to break Colonel Bahar's column in the middle.

'Your forward tanks are surrounded,' Brontke said. 'They can't retreat because they can't pass the Tigers without getting shot out of commission. Your rear guard is now in range of my anti-tank guns. You can't escape without less than seventy percent casualties. It's a complete rout!'

'That appears to be so,' Bahar admitted, bowing stiffly from the waist.

'Appears to be so?' Brontke screeched. 'It is so. It *is* so!' He pounded on the table with his fists. 'A complete victory!' After a moment he straightened up, in control of himself again. 'The morning's exercise is over,' he announced. 'Clear up the simulated battle area. I'll expect you all to hand in your analysis of what Colonel Bahar did wrong by this evening. We may now proceed with the business of the day.'

Lieutenant Khazar, the general's personal aide, who had recently been promoted from corporal when it was discovered that he could read, stepped forward and, standing at stiff attention, read from a clipboard. 'First order of business, at the general's request: a report on the surveillance mission undertaken by Captain Thor last night.'

The captain, wearing a high-altitude

flying suit and carrying his crash helmet, stepped forward and saluted briskly. A small, slender man with wire-rimmed glasses, Captain Thor wore the flying suit — found in the locker room of an airport the legion had overrun — only when he had to report to General Brontke. It would have been useless in his single-prop observation plane, which didn't have any connections for the suit's built-in electrical and oxygen lines. Captain Thor had tried the suit on when he found it out of a vague feeling of jealousy, and he kept it when he discovered that it gave him a sense of increased stature. This was a sense that was very useful when reporting to General Brontke, who tended to diminish whatever stature Captain Thor started with.

'Captain Thor reporting as directed, sir,' he said, holding the salute.

Brontke stared at him steadily, but did not return his salute. 'Well,' he said, 'report.'

Thor lowered his hand slowly to his side, wondering if he looked as foolish as he felt. He decided that it wouldn't be a good idea to remind the general that the last time he had reported he had been chewed out for fifteen minutes for failing to salute. 'I took off at twenty-two hundred hours as ordered and proceeded to my objective,' Thor stated precisely. 'This was an oil pipeline station at grid coordinates six-seventeen slash four-o-four, map thirty-six, in the country of Jeppet. I arrived there by twenty-two thirty and stayed in the area for four hours, until fuel considerations caused me to return.'

'During this time,' General Brontke interrupted caustically, 'did you manage to see anything?'

Captain Thor told himself that he would not let the general's attitude make him angry. After all, what good would it do to get angry? 'The battle between the tribesmen and the Army detachment was already in progress when I arrived,' he announced stiffly. 'I took such pictures as I could to indicate the course of the battle. These photographs are being processed now.'

'Did you see anything worthy of note?'

the general asked. Thor wondered what the general would consider worthy of note; he didn't want to guess wrong. When the general chewed him out for stupidity, as the general had done many times before, even the flying suit didn't help.

'There was one thing,' Captain Thor offered. 'The tribesmen used some sort of heavy weapon to smash down the station's outer wall. It was either a recoilless rifle or an anti-tank gun. I couldn't tell for sure which.'

The general sighed. 'I'll get you silhouette charts to study,' he said. 'Anything else?'

'That's all,' Thor said. 'Shortly after that they overran the station.'

General Brontke nodded. 'The recoilless rifle,' he said, addressing the whole group, 'which we supplied, appears to be doing effective work. The harassing action of — whatever the name of that tribe is . . . '

'El Quarat,' Colonel Bahar said.

'Yes, el Quarat. The harassing action of el Quarat could be quite valuable to us.'

'What are we going to do to prevent their using such weapons against us when we take control?' Colonel Bahar asked. 'After all, they're not exactly on our side either.'

General Brontke allowed himself to smile. 'They'll be out of ammunition by that time,' he said. 'I'm rationing their supply very carefully. They're not going to get nearly as much as they've asked for.'

5

Peter didn't see the helicopter approach until it was settling down among the boxes a few feet from where they were standing. It was a small passenger helicopter with a glass bubble, four seats and pontoons. It bounced lightly up and down where it had landed, as though impatient to be off, and the noise of it drowned out every other sound. The wind of the blades caused a small dust storm and blew bits of paper and debris over the dock.

The side hatch of the helicopter opened and a pointed beard was thrust out. This was followed by a thin face framed by an Arab headdress. The mouth opened, and the beard jiggled up and down in speech, but the words were torn aside by the helicopter wind. No mere human sounds could penetrate that machine-made noise barrier.

'Could that,' Tony shouted, 'be the

good Ali ben Whosis?'

'Sadi ben Dulli,' Peter yelled back. 'It must be.' The beard stopped wobbling, as though realizing that it couldn't be heard, and a white-sleeved arm emerged from the hatch and beckoned. Peter and Tony braced themselves against the hurricane gale and strode over to the helicopter.

'Mister Carthage,' ben Dulli said, extending the hand in greeting.

'Mister ben Dulli,' Peter answered, taking the hand and shaking it.

'This gentleman is a compatriot of yours?' ben Dulli asked.

Peter identified Tony, and ben Dulli formally shook hands with him. 'Go around to the other side of the ship and climb in,' ben Dulli said. 'We're going to take a trip.'

They did as directed, and the copter lurched into the air. Once inside, with the hatch closed, the noise level was endurable. 'Where are we headed?' Peter asked in what approached his normal voice.

'Taking a trip,' ben Dulli said. 'Something I want to show you.'

'What?' Tony asked.

'There was a raid on a pumping station last night. A bit unusual. We want your expert opinion.'

'Good enough,' Peter said. 'Is the Desert Legion raiding already?'

'It's not the legion,' ben Dulli told him. 'Wait till we get there, and I'll show you.'

'All right, it's your show,' Peter said, and contented himself with the air view of Akr he could see through the window. The ancient city was hunched up against the side of the long cliffs that ran along the Gulf, turning into a chain of arid mountains somewhere to the north. From cliffs to Gulf the whitewashed mud-brick buildings, some five to seven stories high, clustered randomly in the bright sunlight. The streets, an improbable maze of winding tracks that started abruptly and ended nowhere, cut the city into odd-shaped segments that looked like the patterns of a mad geometer. An occasional minaret tower, from which the faithful were called to prayer, stuck up out of the jumble.

As the helicopter passed the city and climbed over the cliffs, the scene below

shifted from human disorder to the barren-
ness of the great desert. The sand waste
which claimed so much of the interior of
the vast Arabian peninsula seemed to be-
grudge even the slight habitable strip that
bordered the sea.

'What is that?' Tony asked, pointing out
to the right. Peter turned to look as ben
Dulli tilted the helicopter slightly to give a
better view of what had caught Tony's
eye.

A short distance below them to the
right an ornate eight-sided wall closed off
a portion of land from the desert. The
wall, with tall square towers at each of its
eight corners, and the large domed
building on the inside were covered with
bright patterns of glazework that gleamed
and scintillated in a myriad of colors. The
large part of the closure not taken up by
the building was laid out in an ornate
formal garden, the lush, soft green in
beautiful contrast to the glittering walls.

'The palace,' ben Dulli said. 'Home of
my family for the past four hundred
years.'

'It's fantastic,' Peter said. 'Especially set

off and surrounded by desert like that.'

'It is. It's on the site of a natural oasis.'

'It must be quite a place to live,' Tony said.

'I'd take you down for a visit,' ben Dulli said, 'but we haven't time. Besides, I'm not welcome there.' He jerked the helicopter savagely around and headed it off into the desert.

'Doesn't your brother live there?' Peter asked.

'He does,' ben Dulli agreed. He stared intently at Peter. 'We will be working together, and must trust each other, so I should tell you this, as it affects you and your group, but you must tell no one else. Agreed?'

'Agreed,' Peter said. Ben Dulli turned to Tony, who nodded.

'My brother,' ben Dulli said clearly over the sound of the engine, 'is convinced that I'm trying to kill him.' He looked expectantly at Peter.

Peter nodded and absorbed the information. 'Don't get offended,' he said, 'but are you?'

Ben Dulli smiled without humor. 'A

rational question,' he admitted. 'No, I'm not. I have no reason to, aside from the fact that I happen to be quite fond of him.'

'Why does he think that?' Tony asked.

'I can't blame him,' ben Dulli said. 'The fact is that *someone* is trying. There have been several attempts on his life in the past few months. A group of men tried to ambush him once in the desert, and again three men were found hiding in the palace garden.'

'Can't you find out who did send them?' Peter asked.

'The group in the desert were all killed in the attempt, and none of the three in the garden can be made to talk. They've gone into some sort of trance state that none of our techniques, modern or, er, ancient, can penetrate. It's an interesting puzzle.'

'What makes the Sheik think that it was you who sent them?'

Ben Dulli gave an elaborate shrug that jiggled the control stick and caused the helicopter to yaw in response. 'It's the old doctrine of *cui bono*,' he answered, righting the copter. 'As my brother has no male child, I'm next in line. The thing I can't manage to get through his head is that I've got no interest in ruling Jeppet. I'm quite happy with my present job.'

'That's another point,' Peter said. 'If the Sheik thinks you're trying to kill him, why does he let you keep the job of minister of defense?'

'I'm the most capable person in the Sheikdom of holding that particular post. I went to Sandhurst, you know. My brother doesn't doubt my sincere interest in the welfare of Jeppet.'

'It gets complicated,' Peter said.

'All of that,' ben Dulli agreed. 'Wheels within wheels. What I've told you is, of course, a simplified version of the situation.'

'I'm sure,' Peter said. 'Have you any idea who would want to kill your brother?'

'That's the problem,' ben Dulli said. 'Sheik Abu al-Padl Sulayman ben Ibrahim ben Dull, Al-Rashid, my brother, is an honored and respected man, particularly by his own people. I know of no one who would wish him harm.'

'That's a long name,' Tony commented.

'It's the custom,' ben Dulli explained. 'I left out quite a few.'

'Al-Rashid?' Peter said. 'Isn't that the name of a famous judge?'

'It's the name of quite a few famous people through the years. It's what you would think of as an honorific; it means 'the upright'.'

'How will the Sheik's feelings about you affect us?' Tony asked.

'Well, it will make him suspicious of you, too,' ben Dulli explained. 'After all, it was my idea to bring you here.'

'I see,' said Peter. 'I hope this doesn't get in the way of the job we have to do, which looks impossible enough as it is.'

'I assure you that I will do my best to see that you get every chance,' ben Dulli said stiffly. 'I trust that you will not find it impossible, as the safety, if not the existence, of my country may depend upon what you can accomplish.'

'The difficult we do immediately,' Tony said cheerfully, quoting an old Seabee saying. 'The impossible takes just a bit longer.'

'Time,' ben Dulli reminded him, 'is the one thing we don't have.'

* * *

The helicopter followed an oil pipeline that stretched out in front of them to the horizon, dividing the desert below into two neat halves. After a time a dot appeared at the intersection point and grew into three buildings and a wall as they watched.

'That's the station,' ben Dulli said. Three jeeps and a truck were parked by the wall. Ben Dulli dropped the helicopter neatly beside the lead jeep and silenced the engine.

A Jeppet Army captain ran around to the door of the copter, opened it and stood stiffly at attention as the three men clambered out.

'Captain Mufusti,' ben Dulli growled, 'these are Colonels Carthage and Ryan of War, Incorporated. Feel free to give them any assistance or information they require at any time.'

'Yes, sir,' the captain said.

'What's been happening?'

'We've been checking the extent of the damage and identifying the dead and preparing to move the bodies. We'll load them in the truck.'

'Any survivors?' ben Dulli asked.

'Two. They've been taken out by ambulance, both wounded. Also, two missing.'

'Missing?' The minister of defense sounded shocked. 'What do you mean, missing? Were they buried under the rubble?'

'No, we checked carefully, and they're just not here. Lieutenant Akrat, who was in charge of the detachment, and a representative of the Anglo Jeppet Oil Company named Quinline.'

'Missing,' ben Dulli mused. 'That's something else new. Perhaps el Quarat is developing a whole new system of fighting. Next will be ransom notes.'

'El Quarat?' Peter asked.

'The desert tribe that caused this outrage,' ben Dulli told him.

'What are they like?' Peter asked.

Ben Dulli shrugged. 'They're a nomadic

tribe who travel from wherever they start to wherever they end up in a cyclic pattern. Borders mean nothing to them, and they'll fight to prove it. Their whole mode of existence is based on fighting and sheep stealing. Once every five years or so they show up in the mountains to the north of here, where they stay until the supply of sheep to steal grows too low.'

'Then why would they attack an oil-pumping station?' Tony asked. 'What is there to steal here?'

'That's one of the problems we're going to have to solve. Let me show you another.' He led the way around the corner of the wall to the next side. 'Ah, yes,' he said, 'it's just as Captain Mufusti described it.'

The wall on this side had been one-quarter blown in, and the buildings facing that way were missing sections of front. The ground was thick with rubble.

'There you are, gentlemen,' ben Dulli said. He kicked a section of the wall experimentally, and then jumped back as it collapsed. 'What would cause this?'

'Heavy shelling,' Tony pronounced.

'Bombing?' ben Dulli asked.

'No. Shelling with a heavy-caliber gun. Look at the way only one side has been hit, and there are no roofs missing, only sections of that one roof. If it had been bombs, the destruction would have been less tightly controlled, and the concussion of bombs exploding inside the houses would probably have taken the roofs off.'

The minister of defense shrugged. 'Heavy guns are no more improbable than planes,' he said.

'Can you tell where the gunfire came from?' Peter asked Tony. He turned to ben Dulli.

'There are two possibilities that I can see: light field howitzers, which could be pulled behind a pack animal, or recoilless rifles, which could just about be carried by two men.'

Tony contemplated the debris and picked his way carefully to a building. 'You can eliminate howitzers,' he said. 'Most of them can't depress far enough to get a trajectory this low.' He backed up slowly, studying the target. 'Come here for a minute,' he called. 'I'll show you something.'

Peter walked over with ben Dulli. 'What's your problem?'

'No problem,' Tony told him. 'Solution.'

'What of?'

'Look,' Tony said, 'that building on the left wasn't hit past that point because the building in front was between it and the gun after that. Same thing with the section of wall on the right. That means if you draw a line from the center of those two points and extend it past where we're standing now, it'll reach out to where the gun was.'

'Sounds good,' Peter said. 'Let's go see.'

'Come,' ben Dulli said, 'we'll take the helicopter.' The three of them went back to the helicopter, and ben Dulli again took the controls. With Tony guiding him, he flew slowly in a straight line away from the fort. Peter searched the ground below them carefully as they flew.

'See anything?' Tony asked, as Peter readjusted the binoculars.

'Sand,' Peter said. 'A lot of sand.' They kept on.

'A little to the left,' Tony said. 'There, that's better.'

'That's it!' said Peter. 'There it is.'

'Where?' ben Dulli asked.

'Let down right here so you don't mess up the track. It's a bit more to the left.'

The helicopter lowered to the ground and shut off. Peter jumped out and led the way to his findings. 'Here,' he said. 'Someone's been doing something over here.' He dropped to the ground and dug around for a bit in the sand. 'Aha!' He stood up, pulling a long mailing-tube-like object with him. 'There are probably a lot more around here. It looks like all they did was kick a little sand over them.'

'What is it?' ben Dulli asked.

'The shell casing from a recoilless rifle round. I'd say it's about a one-o-five.' He looked it over carefully. 'No markings on it that I can see.'

Sadi ben Dulli looked unhappy. 'That's bad news,' he said. 'And it still leaves the plane to be explained.'

'What plane?' Tony asked.

'One of the last reports we had by radio from the detachment before they went off the air was that a light plane was circling overhead. That's why I thought of bombs when I heard about the destruction.'

'A light plane couldn't have carried any effective bombs anyhow,' Peter offered.

'True.' Ben Dulli sighed. 'Another mystery.' They walked back to the helicopter and ben Dulli lifted it gently off the sand.

'Look down there,' Peter said as the helicopter gained altitude.

'Where?' ben Dulli asked.

'Over there. Look.' He pointed to the left. 'It seems to be the track of the departing tribesmen.'

Ben Dulli swung the helicopter around. 'I believe you're right. It's the trail of a large group of horsemen heading north.'

'Let's follow it a bit,' Peter suggested.

'We haven't much of a fuel reserve,' ben Dulli said doubtfully.

'Just a short way,' Peter urged. 'They may have dropped something else.'

'Very well.' Ben Dulli tilted the helicopter forward and headed north over the track. 'I never thought of the helicopter as a means of tracking before, but the trail is much more distinct from up here than it would be on the ground.'

'I remember reading somewhere that the American Indians used to climb trees to get a better view of the trail they were following,' Tony said, 'and they were known to be the best trackers in the world.'

'Ah,' ben Dulli said. 'But then, there are so few trees around here.'

'That's true,' Tony admitted.

'Over there,' Peter said, 'seem to be the tracks of a couple of horses which left the main body.' He lifted the binoculars and stared out. 'And there seems to be something over there, by that dune a couple of hundred yards to the left.'

Ben Dulli swung the helicopter around and headed in the direction Peter was indicating.

'There is something,' Peter said after a moment. 'It's a body. It seems to be in uniform.' He tapped ben Dulli on the shoulder. 'I think we've located your missing lieutenant,' he said.

They hovered over the body, which was stretched out on the sand, arms and legs apart, and dropped beside it. 'I think he's been staked out there,' ben Dulli said.

Tony jumped from the machine and went over to the figure. 'You're right!' he called back. He bent over the lieutenant for a second and then stood up. 'Help me cut him loose,' he yelled. 'He's still alive!'

6

The cliffs were old and weathered smooth. They stood as high above the plain as the plain stood above the desert and the sea. It was not thought that anyone lived up there, and there was nothing to attract visitors to the place. Nothing grew except moss and lichens; nothing moved except an occasional rock, split off the face of the cliff by the action of the expanding heat of the day and the contracting cold of the night.

Still, there were signs that man had been there, as man has been to every other inhospitable point on the face of the planet. There was an ancient trail, a track really, that wandered along the face of the cliff, climbing slowly higher and higher. Toward the end of the trail, set into a gap in the rock face of the cliff, there was a stone wall of indeterminable age. The man-size square rocks, which fitted together without mortar as though stacked by the hand of some giant of a bygone race, showed scarcely a crack where they joined. The whole was covered with moss, and looked as though it had been there as long as the cliffs themselves.

On the trail, at the point where it met the ancient wall, stood three men. Two of them were dressed as Arabs and the third, supported by the other two, was in the uniform of the Anglo-Jeppet Oil Company. He stood mute and dull, apparently unaware of anything that was taking place around him.

One of the men gave three closely spaced sounds that approximated the lowing of a camel, and then stood waiting. When nothing happened, he gave the sounds again, louder. Still nothing happened. After a minute he cupped his hands to his mouth and gave three sharp noises that clearly were the bellowing of a camel in great pain. He and his companion watched the top of the wall while the third man stared impassively in front of him.

Still nothing happened.

The spokesman grew angry. He yelled at the wall; he screeched; he threatened;

he implored. Then suddenly he became silent.

A man appeared at the top of the wall. He was dressed in a loose leather jacket and leather leggings worn over coarse wool pants. On top of his close-cropped head there rode a thick leather helmet that fitted tightly over the ears. Without a sound he surveyed the three people below, and then he disappeared.

After a time a wooden pole was swung over the side of the wall. From the pole a wood and straw basket was suspended by a crude pulley arrangement. The basket was lowered by a thick rope. When it reached the ground, the two Arabs helped their companion into it, and one of them climbed in with him. The basket was slowly pulled up the side of the wall and over the top.

★   ★   ★

An ageless man reclined on an ornate couch. His long slender fingers curled around the stem of a water pipe, from which he took long puffs and allowed the blue smoke to curl around his head. His body was motionless and relaxed, but his eyes were never still, the dilated pupils darting about the gloom as though watching great mysteries unfold.

A man entered his presence. 'They have returned, Master.'

For a long time he did not speak; he did not appear to have heard, but then: 'And they brought — ?'

'A young Englishman.'

'Good. Bring him in; he may prove amusing.'

7

In a conference room in the ancient whitewashed building in Akr that housed both the Ministries of Defense and Education, a meeting was in progress. Peter Carthage sat at one end of the highly polished table, and at the other end sat Sadi ben Dulli. In between were the trained and dedicated men of War, Inc., who made up Peter's staff: Tony Ryan, in charge of plans; Eric Jurgens, an expert in all forms of lethal combat, training and weapons; Professor Perlemutter, the stout German with the shrewd mind, head of the propaganda section; John Wander, a young electronics genius, in charge of communications; Bob Alvin, the computer expert, who was said to talk to his machine, and who, some believed, could make it answer him.

'How is your group doing?' Peter asked Eric, who had just started a training program for some of Jeppet's young officers.

Eric, a big blond ex-captain of the Swedish Army, sat with his hands folded in front of him, a deceptively quiet pose. 'They're good boys,' he said. 'In a year I could make fine soldiers of them.'

Ben Dulli moved in his chair. 'We have less than six weeks,' he said, spitting the words out as though each caused him pain.

'Yah,' Eric said, nodding his big head passively, 'that is so.'

'What will you do in six weeks?' ben Dulli demanded.

'What I can,' Eric said.

'Have you finished examining the tanks?' Peter asked Tony.

'I have,' Tony said. 'Seven M four Shermans. Three different models. Six of them will run.'

'What's wrong with the seventh?' ben Dulli asked.

'I'd guess extreme old age. The others suffer from it, too, but not quite as badly. By the way, does anyone know if we have any ammunition for the guns?'

'It was supposed to have been on the ship,' ben Dulli said.

'It doesn't seem to have come off the

ship,' Tony said. 'Oh well, we'll look around for it; it was probably just unloaded in the wrong place.'

'We're not too efficient yet,' ben Dulli admitted. 'The whole idea of Jeppet having an army of its own is brand new. I was minister of police until but a short time ago. A steep price must be paid for independence.'

'That's a fact that people who have independence already tend to forget,' Professor Perlemutter said, 'and so they end up having to pay it all over again.'

'Is it possible to train and equip the Army of Jeppet well enough to fight off the Desert Legion in six weeks?' ben Dulli asked Peter.

'If we had a year, or even six months, there'd be no problem,' Peter replied. 'But six weeks is a little short. We'll have to employ a stratagem.'

'What sort of, er, stratagem?' ben Dulli asked.

Professor Perlemutter leaned forward. 'Trickery and deceit,' he said, chuckling and rubbing his hands together. 'Trickery and deceit, that's what's called for. We'll work out something.'

'If it's at all possible,' Peter assured ben Dulli, 'Herr Professor Perlemutter will figure out how. We have the utmost faith in the professor.'

'That will have to do,' ben Dulli said. 'I've brought along Lieutenant Akrat, the gentleman we found in the desert. He's just been released from the hospital, and I thought you'd want to talk with him.

'Yes,' Peter said. 'Very good; bring him in.'

There was a clicking sound. Peter looked around, but no one else seemed to have heard. He couldn't tell where the sound had come from.

'Ah, Lieutenant,' ben Dulli said as Lieutenant Akrat came into the room, 'come, sit down.'

'Yes, sir.'

'How are you feeling now?' Peter asked.

'Much better than when you first saw me,' Lieutenant Akrat said.

'No doubt,' Professor Perlemutter agreed. 'And now, my boy, would you mind going over for us what happened during that raid?'

There was that sound again, and again no one else seemed to have heard it. Peter thought that it had come from somewhere behind him.

'Not at all, sir,' Lieutenant Akrat said. He started telling the story of the night attack in a clear, low voice.

While he spoke, Peter glanced cautiously around to see what was behind him. It had been a curious, muted, thumping sort of sound. There — there it was again. Peter had located it this time. It was coming from a low cupboard behind him and to his left.

The lieutenant was finishing his report. 'That was about it. After they came through the break in the wall, it turned into a mass of individual engagements. On that level, the outcome of the battle was certain. Our superior firepower became meaningless, and we were outnumbered.' The lieutenant shrugged. 'It took them about twenty minutes to mop us up.'

'Why did you receive special attention from the raiders?' asked Professor Perlemutter.

Peter heard the muted thumping sound again.

'Why did they stake me out in the desert — ? You see,' Lieutenant Akrat explained, 'it's a particularly nasty way to die.'

'Does el Quarat have any reason for wanting you to die in a particularly nasty way?'

'Yes,' Lieutenant Akrat said. He looked up. 'You see, I grew up in that family.'

Professor Perlemutter looked surprised. 'You mean you're a member of el Quarat?'

Lieutenant Akrat nodded. 'I was.'

'You're not anymore?'

'I got wounded in a raid about twelve years ago. At the time, I was twelve years old. I was captured, brought back to Akr and sent to school.'

'I see,' Professor Perlemutter said. 'So they have a special grievance against you.'

'They think I sold them out. For that, there is no excuse.'

'A primitive and direct philosophy,' Professor Perlemutter commented. 'Thank you for your help.'

'You may go now,' ben Dulli said.

The lieutenant stood up. 'Oh, yes,' he said, 'there is one thing else.'

'Yes?'

'After I was left, I would say about an hour later, although that could be way off — it's hard to tell time when you're stretched out on the sand waiting to die — something peculiar happened.'

'What was that?' Peter asked.

'A pair of camels passed close to where I was. I didn't call out because I thought at the time they were from el Quarat; and when I saw they weren't, they were too far away to hear me. It was very strange.'

'What was?' Peter prompted.

'There were three men on the camels: two in Arab dress, and Mister Quinline, the oil company's man.'

'Was he tied up?' asked Professor Perlemutter.

'He didn't appear to be,' the lieutenant said. 'I'm no expert on things like this, but I think he was probably drugged.'

'Drugged?' It was Peter's turn to look surprised.

'Yes, sir. As I say, I'm no expert. He was — how can I say it?' Lieutenant Akrat moved his hands like a man trying to describe a spiral staircase. 'He was dull. Listless. He appeared to have no interest in what was going on around him.'

'I see,' Peter said, not sure that he did. 'Thank you, Lieutenant.'

'Yes, sir. I hope I've helped.' The lieutenant did a neat about-face and left the room.

'He's helped obfuscate matters even worse than they were,' Professor Perlemutter growled.

There was another noise from within the cabinet.

'If you gentlemen — ' ben Dulli started, then stopped in surprise as Peter stood up. Peter motioned him to keep talking. For a second he didn't understand, but then he saw what was happening.

' — would mind waiting here for a second . . . '

Peter yanked open the door to the low cabinet. Inside, crouched almost double, was a short, thin man wearing few clothes and holding a big curved dagger. For a second Peter and the cabinet dweller stared at each other, but then the other man reacted. With a screamed curse, he launched himself out of the cabinet and aimed an underhand swipe of the knife at Peter's midsection.

Peter dropped his two hands in a karate cross chop that sent the knife spinning out of the other's grasp. He continued the follow-through motion, a savage stiff-leg kick that, had it connected, would have broken the collarbone. But it hit only air. His opponent had twisted his body aside and spun around.

Peter whirled and stopped, ready to meet whatever attack the other would launch. His assailant, eyes bulging, glared at Peter and suddenly spat a thin stream of liquid straight into his face.

His eyes and nose stinging, Peter reached forward to grab the skinny body that faced him. He never made it. His arms started jerking spasmodically, and he found himself uncontrollably falling forward. The world started spinning just before he hit the floor.

Peter never completely lost consciousness, but it was a few minutes before he was really aware of what was happening around him. Tony Ryan, having gotten a wet towel from somewhere, was mopping his face; Eric Jurgens had the jack-in-the-cabinet firmly in his iron grasp; and everyone else was rushing around trying to be helpful. From another cabinet across the room, a second surprise guest had been unearthed, but he was putting up no resistance.

Professor Perlemutter, who had not left his chair, was engaged in rapid conversation with ben Dulli. The defense minister's face had assumed a dangerous shade of red.

Peter pulled himself up. The effects of whatever he had been sprayed with seemed to have disappeared, except for continued dizziness and a splitting headache.

'What happened?' Peter asked.

Eric broke the tableau he was holding with his prisoner and twisted the man around and tied his hands behind his back with a piece of electrical wire. 'Little swine!' he barked.

'Look at this,' Tony said, holding up a

small rubber bulb.

Peter took it and examined it. It was hollow, and half-filled with some sort of liquid.

'He had it in his mouth,' Tony explained. 'It's what he squirted you with.'

'I see,' Peter said. He sat down and shook his head. 'Any idea what it is?'

'Not yet,' Tony said. 'Any ill effects?'

'Nothing but a pounding head.'

'Headache?' ben Dulli asked. 'Let me get you something.'

'Never mind,' Peter said. 'I've got something here.' He slid the large ornamental buckle from his uniform belt and twisted it open. In the cavity were a variety of colored pills. 'My portable pharmacy,' Peter explained, seeing ben Dulli's surprised expression. 'We each have one; it's Doctor Steadman's idea.' He selected two pills and gulped them down.

'Excellent notion,' ben Dulli said. 'Allow me to tell you that I'm everlastingly grateful to you for having discovered these two miscreants.'

'My pleasure,' Peter said, hoping the pills would work as fast as they were advertised to.

'Everlastingly grateful,' ben Dulli repeated. 'Do you know what I was starting to tell you when this happened? The Sheik is coming to meet you. In this room.' He shuddered. 'Let's get those two out of here.'

The guards were called into the room, and the two men, who seemed to have retreated into a semi-trance state, were removed, to be held 'at the Sheik's pleasure,' as the ancient phrase has it.

'Would you say the gentlemen were concealed so they might have an opportunity to do bodily harm to His Highness?' Professor Perlemutter asked.

'Yes, I think so,' ben Dulli replied. 'They look just like the men who were caught in the garden. These creatures seem to have an uncanny ability to get into places that are tightly guarded.'

'How do they look like the others?' Peter asked.

'Dressed the same, the same emaciated look, the same glazed-over eyes, the same trance-like state once they're caught. They look like they're seeing something that isn't there for the rest of us. I'd say they were on drugs, but the effect doesn't seem to wear off.'

Professor Perlemutter smiled. 'If it were another time,' he said, 'considering the part of the world we're in, I'd suspect that they were agents of Hasan Sabbah.'

Ben Dulli sighed. 'There are some who say he has returned,' he said. 'I wish I could believe in that legend. It would at least explain things.'

'Hasan Sabbah?' Peter asked.

'It's an old story,' Professor Perlemutter explained, 'part true and part legend, and the two parts have become inextricably mixed. Hasan Sabbah, or the 'Old Man of the Mountain' as his followers and his foes called him, was head of a sect that terrorized most of the Middle East through the eleventh century. He is said to have fed his followers on the leaf of the hemp plant, Cannabis sativa, as botanists know it, to induce visions. The drug, known then as bhang, and today as hashish or marijuana depending on what part of the plant it is extracted from, is one of the oldest known hallucinogens.

'Hasan told his followers that the visions they saw were of paradise, and that they could go to this paradise only by dying in his service. To enhance the visions he kept an inner chamber of his mountain fortress stocked with beautiful hangings, delicious food and lovely, complacent houris. His drugged minions would be placed in this chamber, and heavy, sweet-smelling incense would waft through the rooms. The men would be removed from the rooms in their sleep and told that they had been allowed a brief visit to paradise. They believed.

'Men who were convinced that they had seen and loved the place they were going when they died, provided only that they followed the word of Hasan, would unhesitatingly follow his commands to the death. Hasan used these men to kill anyone who stood in his way and hired them out to other princes. Because of their utter fearlessness, they had an effect out of all proportion to their number. One of them would be more feared than a company of soldiers, because they struck silently, efficiently and totally without fear. These men became known as the 'assassini' — hashish eaters — which is where our word 'assassin' comes from.'

'Quite a story,' Peter said. 'How much of it is true?'

The professor shrugged. 'What is truth?' he asked. 'At any rate, Hasan Sabbah is an historical character. There's some dispute among those who care about such things as to whether the term 'assassin' comes from 'hashish eater,' or 'follower of Hasan,' but the result is the same.'

'It's a romantic story,' Tony said, 'but how does this eleventh-century gangster affect us?'

'As Mister ben Dulli has said,' Professor Perlemutter explained, taking out a long cigar and carefully clipping the end, 'there is a popular legend, or rumor, superstition, old wives' tale or what have you, to the effect that Hasan himself, or someone taking his name, has set up shop somewhere in the mountains.'

'That's what I've heard,' ben Dulli

admitted, 'but I don't see how belief in a nine-hundred-year-old man can have any foundation in fact.'

'I'm a student of superstition,' Professor Perlemutter said. He extracted a gold cigarette lighter from his pocket and went through a ritualistic lighting of his cigar while the others waited for him to continue.

'I'm only allowed five of these a day,' the professor said after a long puff, 'so I attach value to each moment of each cigar. At any rate, I've found that there's usually a basis in fact for every superstition, however warped and twisted it may become, so I feel safe in saying that this one indicates that surely someone, somewhere, is doing something.'

'I'd like to discuss vampires with you when we have time,' Peter said.

'That's rather vague,' ben Dulli said.

'I'll be more specific when I have more facts,' Professor Perlemutter answered. 'As a start, I'd like to examine your various prisoners.'

'That can be arranged,' ben Dulli agreed, 'but they'll tell you nothing.'

'I don't doubt you. But perhaps the

manner of their silence will be instructive.'

Ben Dulli stared at the professor, then looked at each of the others in turn, as if to see whether he could read the meaning of Perlemutter's cryptic statement in their eyes. Then he gave it up. 'As you say.'

The door opened and two non-Army guards in traditional Arab dress with rifles strapped to their backs came in. After them came an English brigadier and Sheik ben Dulli, known as Al-Rashid. Unlike his brother, who was in Arabian robes, the Sheik wore a well-tailored Western suit. Only his headdress, of white cloth with twisted fine gold thread and a solid gold band, was native to Jeppet. He was smaller than his brother, his features finer and more precise, and he had dark, intent eyes that burned strongly from deep-set eye sockets.

The group stood up, but the Sheik waved them back to their seats. 'Let's keep this as informal as possible,' he said in a clipped British accent. He took an empty chair in the middle of the long table. The brigadier sat beside him, and the two guards placed themselves close behind the chair.

'I understand you had a bit of excitement in here before I arrived,' the Sheik said, eying his brother.

Ben Dulli nodded. 'That's so.'

'Yes,' the Sheik said. 'Let me introduce Brigadier General Smyth Black, commander of the British garrison in Akr, and head of the British military forces in Jeppet. General, these are the men of the War, Incorporated group that my brother has sent for. I'll have to let them introduce themselves, since this is the first time I'm meeting them.'

Al-Rashid, Peter decided, didn't sound exactly hostile; he was waiting to be shown. *Well*, Peter thought, *we'll have to show him.* 'Peter Carthage,' he started, 'colonel in charge.'

'Tony Ryan, colonel, plans.' Tony picked it up, and so it continued around the rest of the table.

The brigadier nodded after the last name. 'It's a pleasure, gentlemen,' he said. 'I've heard a lot about you, most of it good. I have instructions from Her

Majesty's Government to give you all the aid I can, but I'm afraid it won't be too much. As of May first we're to be entirely moved out.'

'What sort of help can you give us?' Peter asked.

'What do you need?' the brigadier countered, fingering his walrus mustache.

'Tanks, tank destroyers or anti-tank guns.'

'Quite right,' Smyth-Black said. 'I can give you something along that line, but not very much. Still, every little bit and all that sort of thing.'

'Anything you could give us would help,' Peter agreed.

'Yes, well. Upon leaving we're prepared to transfer our armored brigade, lock, stock and treads, to the Army of Jeppet. For a price to be agreed upon by our governments, naturally. The brigade con- sists of four Centurion battle tanks.'

'Four?' Tony asked.

'Small brigade,' Smyth-Black admitted.

'I won't complain,' Tony said. 'Is that the Centurion with the one-o-five- millimeter gun?'

The brigadier looked slightly embarrassed. 'Again I must disappoint you. These are the Number Eights, with the twenty-pounders. Nothing but the second-best.'

'We're grateful for all assistance the British Government can give us,' the Sheik said firmly.

'Oh, yes,' Smyth-Black said, 'one other thing, if it will help. We've discovered, in the process of cleaning out our military warehouses, one old General Grant and a bale of spare parts that we're quite willing to, er, leave behind by accident. We can't sell it to you, as we can't account for it ourselves.'

'General Grant,' Tony mused. 'If I remember correctly, that's the American-made M-three, isn't it?'

'I believe so,' the brigadier said.

'I think a lot of the parts are interchangeable with the M-four, given the proper application of sweat and ingenuity. Yes, we could use that, thank you.'

'Very good,' the brigadier said. 'And we have quite a bit of reconnaissance information on the Desert Legion. Keeping tabs on them ourselves, you know.

We'll sort of leave that behind also.'

'That,' Peter said, 'would be very nice.'

'I don't suppose that you could see your way clear to leaving behind a few of those Hornet-Malkaras I saw parked in your garrison?' Tony asked.

'Hornet who?' ben Dulli asked.

'Hornet-Malkara,' the brigadier said. 'It's one of our latest anti-tank systems. A sort of armored car with four rockets on the back. Very effective, and in limited supply. I don't think Her Majesty's Government would approve of our giving any away.'

'It was just a thought,' Tony said.

'I'll see what I can do,' the brigadier promised, 'but wouldn't you prefer the Stone of Scone? I think I'd have a better chance.'

'Well,' Tony said, 'I guess we could throw it at them.'

'Does your reconnaissance information indicate how many armored vehicles the Desert Legion has?' Peter asked.

'I'm not sure of the exact figure,' Smyth-Black said, 'but I believe the number is somewhere around forty.'

Eric sat up straight. 'Forty!' he boomed.

'Yes. Impressive, isn't it? I wouldn't wonder but they are receiving some sort of outside aid.' He got up and tucked his swagger stick firmly under his arm. 'Well, I wish you luck.'

8

On a small plain sandwiched between the mountains to the north of Akr, el Quarat made camp. The tents gathered around in a wide circle and enclosed livestock, children and dogs. There was only one entrance to the area: through a narrow, well-guarded pass. A battle-gray four-ton truck had just finished threading its way between the boulders and the riflemen in the pass and was entering the plain.

To Captain Thor, who was bouncing in the seat to the right of the driver, the scene was unbelievably primitive. Captain Thor was an avid reader of Westerns, usually in French translation (which, due to some difference in the language, always seemed to be a bit bloodier), and except for a few minor differences in the shapes of the tents, the garb of the men and the vehicle he was in, he felt he was living a scene in one of the books. He even knew which scene: the one where the renegade settler is bringing guns to sell to the Indians.

The driver of the truck steered it between two goats and an unhappy dog and stopped it within the circle of tents. There were, Thor observed, no women in sight. They must have scurried inside the tents at the first sound of the approaching truck. The men, however, were there: sitting, singly and in pairs, in front of the tents. The few that weren't cleaning and polishing their wicked-looking long rifles were sharpening knives and swords. They were all staring at him, but none of them made any move to come over to the truck. Thor leaned unhappily back into the corner of his seat. The Indians, he reflected, usually ended up killing and scalping the renegade settler. He passed his hand lovingly over his balding head.

'You'd better get out, sir,' the driver suggested helpfully, keeping his hands on the steering wheel and his eyes straight ahead as if to remind Thor that he was only a driver. 'They seem to expect it.'

Thor glared at him, but it did no good. 'Yes. Expect it. Naturally. Can't do business from the seat of a truck. Have to talk to the natives.' Wishing he'd brought his flight suit, Thor pulled on a pair of white linen gloves and stepped out of the truck.

On the ground, where he had to deal with people on their own level, Thor always felt very short. Much shorter than his five-foot-six would warrant. He made up for this by being nasty to his inferiors and obsequious to his betters. When in doubt, he tended toward obsequiousness. In the present circumstances, he felt, looking around the camp, neither of his habitual attitudes would do. He'd have to strike a balance.

'Hem,' he said.

The men kept polishing.

'I am Captain Thor,' he announced. No one answered.

'I represent General Brontke.'

Someone spat on the ground. Thor wasn't sure whether it was a comment or not. He decided to ignore it. 'I bring you supplies.'

One of the men got up and entered a tent. That might be a good sign. Thor considered it. He decided it might also be a bad sign. The natives, Colonel Bahar had told him, were very touchy. He wished he'd thought to ask what they were touchy about.

After a nervous minute a tall, impressive man strode out of the tent. 'I am Mondar,' he said in English, staring down at Thor.

'Mondar,' Thor repeated. Then he remembered that that was the chief's name. 'It is a pleasure to meet you, Honored Sir,' he finished.

'You have something for me?'

'Yes, Honored Sir. There are crates of supplies in the back of the truck.'

The tall man nodded stiffly and clapped his hands. He said something in a language Thor didn't understand, and three men put down their rifles and walked casually over to the rear of the truck. The driver got out and lowered the tailgate for them.

'You will have tea with me while the truck is being unloaded,' Mondar said. It didn't sound like a question, so Thor followed him back to the tent.

Mondar pulled open the flap and stood

aside for his guest. Thor scuttled past him and stood in what seemed complete darkness after the glare of the sun. He wondered what Mondar wanted. In his experience, everyone always wanted something. He wondered, as he had often during the drive, why he had been detailed for this delivery. No assignment, in his mind, was ever purely routine until it was over. Perhaps Mondar had instructions from General Brontke to get rid of him. In the books he read, things like that were always happening. He heard Mondar move behind him, and he involuntarily tightened his shoulder muscles.

'Please sit down, Mister Thor,' Mondar said.

'Captain,' Captain Thor corrected. He could just make out a bulky object on the floor to his right, and he moved over to it and sat down. It sank under his weight and he was almost thrown over backward. Righting himself, he discovered he was sitting on a cross between a pillow and a cushion. He took off his gloves, stuck them in his belt and touched the cross. It felt like silk.

Mondar sat down opposite him and snapped his fingers. A small boy appeared from behind a drape.

Thor thought there was something funny about the boy's appearance but couldn't figure out what it was in the dim light. Mondar said something and the boy disappeared.

Thor had heard that no Arab would ever harm anyone who was his guest, and thus under his protection. He was trying to remember at what point this guest status was established. Was drinking tea enough, or did you have to break something? Oh yes, bread. You had to break bread. He looked around but didn't see any bread.

'I welcome you as a guest to my house,' Mondar said.

Thor sighed, relaxed and forgot about the bread. 'Thank you,' he said. 'Thank you very much.'

'We shall drink tea together, and I will tell you of el Quarat, and you will tell me of the Desert Legion and your General Brontke, whom I have heard much about.'

'Yes,' Captain Thor said. 'I'd like that.'
So what Mondar wanted was information; that he could understand. He found
that his eyes were beginning to adjust to
the dim light, and he could make out
some of the details of the tent. It was
quite a tent. The drapes, hanging from
the side walls, were woven in an intricate
pattern of gold, blue and brown. The rug
that lay over the sand was of many colors
and incredibly deep. Even the tent poles
were covered with richly woven fabric.

'You admire my tent?' Mondar asked,
seeing him gazing around.

'Those drapes must be worth a
fortune,' Thor answered. This was his
highest, and most sincere, form of praise.

'I imagine,' Mondar said, shrugging.
'They're quite old.'

The boy returned, carrying a small
silver tray. Thor's eyes were well enough
adjusted to see what was peculiar about
the boy's appearance. The boy was one of
the most beautiful young girls that he had
ever seen. Thor judged her age to be
about sixteen. He couldn't see her face
because she was wearing a veil, but he

could watch her hands. They put the tray down and removed two cups, putting one at each end of the low table. The cups were fine British bone china, well over a hundred years old and beautiful in their own right, but Thor didn't notice.

The hands picked up the teapot, which was also of silver and shaped like a dolphin that had somehow decided to become a teapot. It was priceless, a fact that would have interested Thor, but he couldn't see its value.

He watched the hands. Fine hands, slender hands, they moved like birds, pouring the tea and dropping in the un-dissolvable lumps of rock-hard sugar.

Thor took the cup of tea, stirred the sugar rock around and covertly watched the girl. He discovered that the fine silk garment that covered her body changed shape as she moved, pressing against the delicate skin here and swirling away from it there. With the aid of his imagination, Thor was able to picture the body that moved beneath the silk. On some subjects Thor had a good imagination.

The girl bowed to the two men and

backed out of the room. In his imagination Thor pursued her. She waited shyly for him. With hands that trembled slightly, he lifted her veil. The small, perfect face looked trustingly up at him. Her lips pouted to be kissed . . .

'You do not drink your tea, Captain Thor.'

Thor came back to earth. 'What? I mean, sorry. I was waiting for it to cool slightly.'

'Yes, of course,' Mondar said, sipping his tea slowly and staring.

Thor brought his cup to his lips and took a gulp of the searing hot liquid. 'Good tea,' he said. 'Excellent tea.'

'Yes?' Mondar said. 'Tell me, do you know General Brontke well?'

'A close friend,' Thor assured the chieftain. 'Known him for years. We trust each other implicitly.'

'Yes?' Mondar asked. He followed with a series of questions about Brontke. They went from the personal to the specifically military, concentrating on the general's method of handling men.

Thor wanted Mondar for a friend. It

was important for him to be well thought of by the desert chieftain. Thor planned to visit Mondar — and that girl — again. He answered the questions as well as he could. When he didn't know the answer, which was often, he made it up. Thor had never known he could speak so well. Mondar seemed impressed. Thor wondered whether the girl was listening from behind the drapes. He hoped so. It didn't occur to him that she probably didn't speak English.

In the middle of a lengthy explanation of how General Brontke called on Thor for advice whenever he had a problem, which was so convincing Thor almost believed it himself, the discussion was interrupted. A slim elderly man with a slight beard pulled aside the curtain and whispered a few guttural words to Mondar.

'So,' said Mondar. 'Thank you, ben Sinna.' The man nodded and left the tent.

'The supplies are unloaded,' Mondar told Thor softly. 'All of them.'

'Ah,' said Thor brightly.

'But they don't seem to be all there,'

Mondar continued.

'Oh?'

Mondar stood up, towering over Captain Thor. 'What sort of game is your general playing?' he demanded.

'I, er, don't know what you mean.'

'We were promised machine guns,' Mondar told him. 'Our great need is machine guns. We were waiting for machine guns. We didn't get machine guns.'

'There must have been some mistake,' Thor suggested weakly.

'Come with me,' Mondar said, and strode out of the tent. With one last hopeless glance at the curtain behind which the girl had disappeared, Thor followed.

They stopped by the side of the truck, where many cases of supplies were stacked on the ground. Mondar went to each case and examined it. 'Rifle cartridges,' he said. 'Bandages, dynamite, tinned food and a few shells for the recoilless rifle. But no machine guns.' He turned to Thor. 'Can you explain the lack?'

Captain Thor was a little bit nervous to find out he had been carrying dynamite, and a lot more nervous that he hadn't been carrying something this explosive chieftain had been expecting. 'N-no,' he said, 'I c-can't.'

'Bah!' Mondar yelled. 'O adviser to General Brontke, your general is playing false with us. We kept our part of the bargain and attacked and destroyed the station. He has not lived up to his part. He has not sent half of the recoilless rifle ammunition we were to get, and he has sent no machine guns. I shall no longer trust him. You may send this word back.'

Grateful to discover that this meant Mondar was letting him go back, Thor hastily agreed. 'It must be some sort of mistake,' he said. 'An error on the part of the men who loaded the truck. I will personally see that it's rectified.' He tried to smile at Mondar, and managed to bare a few teeth below a tight upper lip. 'You have my word.'

Mondar stared curiously at him, and he quickly climbed up into the truck. 'Come on, put that thing down and let's get out of here,' he snarled at the driver, who had been patiently reading a comic book.

The men of el Quarat watched the

truck leave as impassively as they had watched it arrive.

★ ★ ★

While the driver guided the truck around and over the convolutions in the road leading away from the camp, Captain Thor bounced and sulked. He had been betrayed; there was no other explanation. General Brontke had deliberately left the requested machine guns off the shipment, hoping that Mondar would blame Thor. If there had been any other reason for it someone would have told him that the guns weren't there. It didn't occur to Thor that the only reason Mondar had blamed him was the twenty minutes he had spent posing as Brontke's right-hand man.

I wouldn't go back, Thor told himself, *if I had anywhere else to go.*

As though in answer to his thoughts, 'anywhere else' was provided. The truck came to a sudden, skidding stop. Thor's head went forward into the ashtray. 'What,' he yelped, pulling his head free,

103

'do you think you're doing?'

'Stopping,' the driver told him. 'There's a log across the road.'

'Oh,' Thor said, peering out over the windshield. Sure enough, the grandfather of all trees had fallen across the road. 'How are we going to move that?'

'I don't think we'll have to,' the driver said, pulling his carbine out from under the seat.

'What do you mean?'

'How'd the log get there?' the driver asked. He kept fishing under the seat. 'Hell! I can't find the clip.'

Thor looked puzzled. 'It fell. How else?'

'From where? There aren't any trees growing around here.'

'Oh,' Thor said. He looked around. 'You're right.'

'Take out your pistol,' the driver said. 'I can't find the clip for this carbine.'

Thor pulled the Mauser from his belt holster and looked sadly at it. 'It's not loaded,' he admitted.

The driver swore explosively.

The door on the driver's side was

opened from the outside, and Thor shrank back in his seat. Then the door on his side was opened. A short man with a leather skull-cap grinned up at him. 'What do you want?' Thor screeched.

The man spat a thin stream of liquid that broke on Thor's nose and washed over his face.

'Hey!' Thor yelped. He tried to get up and fell forward into oblivion.

9

The ground was flat and fairly level, barren except for an occasional stunted bush or clump of moss, and dry. What changes there were in the level of the land were not gradual hills or slopes, but sudden: the quick drop of a gully where an ancient river had dug its way across the rocky land, or the sharp rise of a cliff, jagged against the sky. This was the desert. Most of the desert is like this, and it reaches far away in every direction. The sandy wasteland with eternally shifting dunes is only a small part of this Great Desert.

Peter Carthage took off the wide-brimmed Australian campaign hat that was shielding his face from the sun and mopped his forehead. 'This is a hell of a place to fight a war,' he said.

'I agree,' said Eric Jurgens. 'You, at least, commute. I have to stay out here with the troops, war-weary and hungry for news from home. Also chocolate cake and hand-knitted socks.'

'I saw that movie,' Peter said.

'Me too,' Eric agreed. 'All twelve of it. What's new in Akr?'

Peter thought for a minute. 'Well, they're hooking up new air conditioners at the rate of thirty a day. It's in all the papers.'

'A splendid notion,' Eric said, 'which I will not mock.'

'Also, Miss Quinline has come to town.'

'Who?'

'Miss Quinline. The sister of the oilman who disappeared in the raid. She's come to find her brother. All very romantic and Victorian.'

'Yah!' said Eric. 'The woman enters the story. What's she like?'

'I can't tell you. I haven't met her. Her picture is very pretty.'

Erie shook his head sadly. 'You're getting slow, not at all the dashing young skirt chaser you once were.'

'I,' Peter announced, 'have shouldered my responsibilities. Nose to the wheel, shoulder to the grindstone, head firmly on the ground, I assume the position of an adult.'

'Something like that,' agreed Eric. 'How's the training coming?'

'Well, the tank drivers now know how to drive tanks, the gunners have a rough idea of how to shoot the guns, the loaders usually manage to load the guns, and the commanders now can give commands. Unfortunately they're not yet clear on just what commands to give, but that takes time. Also, the mechanics — they've had possibly more training than anyone else in the past two weeks.'

'How would they do on a battlefield?' Peter asked.

Eric shrugged his wide shoulders. 'In a fair fight against well-trained troops, they'd get killed. Knowing how to drive a tank or shoot a gun doesn't make a tank fighter out of you. These men have never been in combat, at least not in tank combat. It's not a question of personal ability or bravery; it demands teamwork and an exact knowledge of what the machine under you can do. As well as the machine on your right and the tank commander in it. It would also help to know what the enemy machines can do and, if possible, what they probably will do. These men have just not had the experience in working together that makes for good teamwork.'

'How long would it take them to get it?' Peter asked.

'A year of good, solid training, and then six months in the field on maneuvers and I'd trust them against Rommel's Panzer Corps.'

'Eighteen months? We don't even have eighteen weeks.'

'I know. If you could get me four months of training time I'd feel good about sending them against the Desert Legion. I wouldn't want to send them against a troop of boy scouts on less than that.'

'Unfortunately there's no stalling action I know that we can depend on to work,' Peter said. 'When the legion decides to attack is when we defend.'

'Well,' said Eric, 'we'll do what we can.'

'I have faith,' Peter said. 'Would you like to fly back to Akr with me and watch a presentation?'

'What sort of presentation?'

'We're going to show the powers-that-be our battle plan.'

Eric slapped Peter on the back. 'Splendid. I'd love to go. I didn't know we had a battle plan.'

'It's just a little something Tony and the Professor and I whipped together between Mahjongg games during these hot afternoons.'

'How about that?' Eric asked.

'That's what I say,' Peter said. They climbed into the light plane Peter had borrowed to fly out to the desert camp, and Peter took off and headed east, toward Akr.

The plane landed on hard-packed sand outside the Sheik's palace, and an old Packard drove up to take them inside.

'A beautiful car,' Eric said, stretching out across his side of the seat. 'It has leg room. They don't make them like this anymore. Do you know what year it is?' he asked the chauffeur.

'The date of manufacture of this automobile was nineteen hundred and thirty-six,' the chauffeur informed them.

He was a short dark man who sat proudly in his blue suit and peaked hat.

'It's a beautiful machine,' Eric repeated. 'When it's gone there'll be nothing like it left.'

'Beg pardon, sir,' the chauffeur said, leaning back but keeping his head carefully front, eyes on the sand, 'but when this car is gone there are eighteen others just like it that have never been used.'

'Never been used?' Peter asked.

'Eighteen?' Eric demanded.

'Yes,' the chauffeur said. 'There were originally fifty, but at the rate of one a year, which is how they've been used, there are only eighteen left now. The Sheik — the old Sheik, that is, father of our Sheik — bought fifty identical cars when he was on a trip to the United States of America, and they have been using them at the rate of one a year.'

'He must have liked the car,' Peter said.

'Yes, sir. Also, I understand he was angry at the British company that had been supplying him with automobiles. He had been buying ten every two years.'

'Perhaps he tired of conspicuous consumption,' Peter offered.

'He was never sick a day in his life,' the chauffeur insisted. Peter let it go.

They drove through the gates of the palace and circled the garden, pulling up by the wide doors to the main building.

'Those steps and columns are marble,' Eric said.

'I wouldn't be a bit surprised,' said Peter.

'I'll bet there isn't any marble quarried within a thousand miles of here.'

'That wouldn't surprise me either.'

'Ah, well,' Eric said, 'in some ways it's nice to have money.'

Dulli met them by the doors and guided them through corridors and court-yards to a large bare room. A blackboard at the head of the room faced a large group of folding chairs. Seated in the chairs were the War, Inc. mission and the government and military leaders of Jeppet.

Eric and the defense minister sat down, and Peter went to the front of the room to face the group. 'Good afternoon, Your Highness,' he said, nodding to the Sheik.

112

'And good afternoon, gentlemen. We are met here today to discuss the tentative plan we have arrived at to meet the immediate menace of the Desert Legion. As the British military presence will leave Jeppet in four weeks, that takes precedence over any long-range plans.'

He turned to the blackboard. 'The situation, as revealed to us by the reconnaissance photographs taken by the British, is this. Here,' he said, making an X on the board, 'is the legion, with a force of some forty tanks. Here is Akr.' He drew another X. 'Between are some three hundred miles of desert and the sixteen tanks that Jeppet will be able to muster.' He paused to see what effect his words were having. The Sheik was staring gloomily at the blackboard. Ben Dulli was watching Peter intently, as though waiting for the rabbit to be pulled out of the hat.

Peter took a firm mental grip on the imaginary hat. 'There's a way to beat them,' he said. 'Or, more accurately, a way to let them defeat themselves. Colonel Ryan came up with the basic idea, and Professor Perlemutter added the necessary embellishments, so I'll let them explain it to you.'

Peter sat down and Tony stood in his place. He went to the blackboard and added a straight line to the right of the Xs and a wavy line between. 'Like all good ideas,' he said, 'this one is basically simple.'

'What are the lines?' asked ben Dulli.

'Yes, well, I'll get to that. This line,' he said, touching the straight line, 'is the coast, and the other represents the mountains.'

'It isn't very accurate,' a Jeppet Army officer commented.

'As long as it gets the basic idea across,' Tony said. 'Now look.' He fished into a briefcase on his chair and pulled out some photographs. 'These are the recon photos of the Desert Legion.' He handed them around. 'Does anybody recognize those squarish dark objects?'

'Tanks?' the Jeppet officer hazarded.

'Right,' Tony agreed. 'Not only that, but I'll tell you what sort of tanks. They're Soviet-made T-thirty-fours.'

The Sheik took one of the photographs

and stared at it. He got up and moved directly under the light, tilting the photograph in different ways to eliminate the glare. Then he ran his thumbnail across the picture and looked again. 'Excuse me for a second,' he said, and handed the picture to ben Dulli, saying something to him in a low voice. Ben Dulli nodded and squinted at the picture. After a moment he gave up and passed it to Peter.

'Those black dots,' ben Dulli said, 'are tanks?'

Peter examined the picture. It was mostly white, with a scattering of gray lines and squarish black dots spread across it. There was a small block of hand-lettered numbers and letters in the lower left-hand corner. 'Not all tanks,' he said. 'Some trucks and tents, too.'

'This you can tell from the photograph?' the Sheik asked.

'It takes practice,' Peter admitted.

'You can even say what sort of tank it is?'

'No,' Peter said, 'I couldn't, but Colonel Ryan could.'

The Sheik took the photograph back from Peter and stared at it again. He held it close to his eyes and then far away. 'I realize this is not the point,' he said, 'and I don't want to appear as if I doubt you, but I think it's close to miraculous that you can tell anything from this piece of abstract art.'

'I can demonstrate how it's done, if you like, Your Highness,' Tony offered. The Sheik looked interested and sat down.

Peter leaned back in his chair, his long legs sprawled out in front of him, and hoped that the demonstration was convincing. Anything that could help convince the Sheik that War, Inc. was a very capable organization was good and proper at this point. The scheme with which War, Inc. intended to preserve Jeppet for the Jeppetians was comparatively subtle. It might be hard to sell the tradition-oriented Jeppet brass — a group that included the Sheik and his brother. Peter's fear was that the Jeppet military would insist on a direct defense, which would be suicide.

Tony swiveled the blackboard around, revealing a white screen on the other side.

He beckoned to an aide on the side of the room, who wheeled a large, bulky black object to the center. 'This is a positive image projector,' Tony said. 'We use it as a training aid.' He put the photograph under a glass plate in the gadget and flipped a switch. 'Would someone get the lights?'

The room was thrown into darkness, and Tony focused the image on the screen. Peter heard a motion and turned. One of the guards had casually seated himself between the Sheik and ben Dulli. A certain lack of trust, Peter decided.

'This is an aerial photograph of the legion's encampment in the desert,' Tony said. 'The information block in the corner gives us data on the photograph itself'. He produced a pointer from somewhere and tapped a zero. 'The first number shows that it was taken from directly overhead. The next gives longitude and latitude as best as can be estimated, which is usually pretty good. The next tells that it was taken at fifteen hundred hours, or three p.m., local time. The next line is the altitude, twelve thousand feet, or about two miles. The rest is camera and film processing data, which we can ignore for now. Let's just see what we can get out of this much.

'Now for the picture itself. The first step is to pick out something we can positively identify. A man standing in the desert, in a picture taken straight down from two miles up, will show up as a small black dot, if he shows up at all. However, at three in the afternoon he'll cast a distinct shadow. Since the sun at this time of year will be forty-eight degrees from the vertical at three, the shadow of a five-foot-six man will be just about six feet long. The scale of the photograph, given the lens used, would make six feet the length of this mark.' He indicated a thin black line in the photograph with his pointer. 'To confirm this,' he said, pointing to a cluster of such lines near a larger black square, 'we have here a group of men.'

'Very good,' the Sheik applauded. 'Excellent logic.'

'It gives us a start,' Tony admitted. 'Now then, this thing the men are near.

Since this is, fortunately, a desert, which simplifies the work a bit, we can assume it isn't a natural formation. Also, its shape is too regular. The group of men are apparently either approaching or departing from it. It is, therefore, most probably a tent. Its height, as shown by the shadow, works out to fourteen feet. We can further conclude that it's a large tent. Since the shape and size of military tents are fairly standardized — most of them are U.S. Army surplus anyway — we can judge the exact size of this particular tent. It's too large for a command tent, and is probably the mess area.'

He indicated another area. 'Now these things over here, as you should be able to tell now that you have an idea of the relative size of objects in the picture, are trucks. The shape is quite distinctive.'

'Yes, of course!' Sheik Al-Rashid sounded as excited as a small boy learning to make words out of letters. 'And that must be a staff car or a jeep. And that over there — by Allah, that's an airplane.'

'I don't see it,' ben Dulli grumbled.

'It takes a certain kind of eye,' Tony

said. 'Some people get the hang of it faster than others. In some ways it's more an art than a science.' He nodded to the Sheik. 'You're right, sir.'

Tony pointed to several objects scattered throughout the picture. 'These are the tanks. They aren't lined up in neat rows for us to examine, of course, but judging by bulk and height, we can make them out.' He pointed to one of them. 'This one has presented a neat profile to the sun and cast a beautiful shadow for us to examine. Here are body, turret and gun. You can even tell that the gun has no muzzle brake on the end.

'This one gives us exact size and general profile. By comparing it with bits and pieces of the profiles of some of the others, a process which takes many hours, we can draw a detailed picture of the tank.' He pulled the photograph from the glass and slid a line drawing in its place. 'This is the result of those hours of work. We also had other photographs taken at different angles and times to use.'

'I see,' said the Sheik, who was completely convinced. 'It's like a magical effect: an astounding result produced by intense, detailed preparation.'

Peter said, 'It's just that. Except in this case we're quite willing to explain the trick. Something you don't understand might be more impressive, but you're never quite sure it can be duplicated.'

'I'm quite willing now to believe you can do anything you say you can,' said the Sheik.

Peter crossed his fingers and hoped the aura would last.

'The tank,' Tony persisted, 'is now identifiable by its profile drawing. Fairly high, squat design, with a large turret placed well forward, bulging fore and aft. No muzzle brake on the gun. This, so far, could apply to several tanks, but we also know the exact size. Then there's the placement of military features: machine gun here, spare fuel cans on the rear side.

'We now review the few vehicles left that this could be by using the test of reasonable access. Could the Desert Legion be expected to have acquired them anywhere? After eliminating the 'no' answers to that, we're left with the

T-thirty-four.' He turned off the machine and had the lights switched on.

One of the Jeppet Army colonels leaned forward and whispered something to ben Dulli. The defense minister nodded and looked up. 'You seem to have made your point,' he said to Tony, 'and it was well done.' He shifted in his chair, looking worried. 'But tell me, how important is it? We knew they were using some medium tank, and that they have about forty of them. How does knowing the so-to-speak brand name help?'

'Knowing your enemy is always helpful,' Tony said, 'and the more you know about him the better. In this case the information is essential to our plan.' He turned the screen back around to its blackboard side. 'So, here we are. And here's the Desert Legion with its forty or so T-thirty-four tanks. How does the knowledge help us — ?

'We're agreed on one thing: that the legion is going to attack us as soon after the British pull out as possible. For one thing, they couldn't be where they are for any other reason. They're even willing to give up the chance of a surprise attack to wait there, which indicates they think it's more important to give us as little time to prepare as possible. The advance will probably be within days, or perhaps hours, of the time the British troops leave.

'How will they attack? That's the big question right now. Since they have no hope of surprise, and since they must know we can put up little resistance, their best bet would be to race straight through the desert to Akr. Jeppet, as both we and they must realize, is Akr. Once it's taken they have only to wipe up the garrison at Port Hornblower and any units left in the desert, and they've won. Before government protests could bring aid from any foreign power, there'd be a new government. Great Britain is the only state with enough at stake in Jeppet to rush aid, and by the decolonization agreement, they're the one state that can't intervene.'

'That is so,' Sheik Al-Rashid stated, his voice unable to hide the strong overtones of anger and grief. 'And a people who have their first chance to emerge from poverty in fifteen hundred years will see it snatched from them.'

Ben Dulli rose and silently put his hand on his brother's arm, and no one moved to separate them. Al-Rashid looked up and searched his brother's face. They stayed, locked eye to eye, for a moment, and something unspoken seemed to pass between them, as it can sometimes between blood brothers, no matter how great their misunderstanding.

Al-Rashid made a decision. 'Come sit by me, my brother,' he said, 'and let us face this thing together.' The guard changed seats, and brother sat beside brother.

A few of the officers in the room showed immediate signs of relief. It must have been a great strain, Peter realized, to have their two leaders separated by suspicion.

'If what you say is true,' ben Dulli said to Tony, 'and we cannot win, we must die trying. But we can't ask you to join us.'

'I don't think it's quite that bad,' Tony said. 'That, remember, is Brontke's ideal plan — or we're assuming it is. However, he has T-thirty-four tanks, and that makes a difference.'

'How?' the Sheik asked.

'The range of action of the T-thirty-four tank is slightly under two hundred miles. With auxiliary fuel drums, this can be stretched to almost three hundred miles. That means that without additional fuel the forty tanks of the Desert Legion would be stranded somewhere outside of Akr. Without its tanks, the Desert Legion becomes a force of some two thousand fighting men, enough to cause trouble, perhaps, but not to take over a country.'

'This is true,' the Sheik said. 'Your words bring hope.'

'Can't they get this additional gasoline?' ben Dulli asked.

'There are several ways,' Tony said, 'that we'll go over in order. 'First: they might use half of the tanks to carry fuel for the other half, thus having twenty tanks arrive at Akr quite able to fight. Second: they can establish caches of fuel out in the desert for their vehicles to fill up. Third: they can plan, by some means, to have additional fuel waiting for them when they arrive here. The one thing the city of Akr doesn't lack is a gasoline supply. Fourth: they can simply bring up the gasoline on trucks, of which they have a sufficient number. Can anyone think of any methods not outlined in those four?'

'Aren't they sufficient?' a colonel asked.

'We'll go over them, but first let's see if anyone can think of one we've overlooked.'

'Couldn't they,' a general asked cautiously, 'just tap one of our pipelines? They run as far as seventy miles out into the desert.'

Peter identified the questioner as General Ashmed, ranking officer in the Army.

'They could,' Tony admitted, 'but they'd get crude oil, not anything to put in an engine.'

'Ah,' General Ashmed said, 'true, very true.'

'Excuse me,' a major said, 'but what about a tanker lying off the coast fifty miles up or so? It could pump oil right ashore.' Peter noted the red piping on the major's uniform that indicated he was general staff, and decided to find out his name. It was an intelligent question.

'We thought of that,' Tony said, 'but discounted it for several reasons. Few ships carry pumps of their own big enough to get any volume ashore; the tanks can't cross the mountains to reach the sea any farther than eight miles away from Akr; and it would take too long even if they did have some secret way.

'Any others?' Tony looked around. 'Okay, back to my original four. The first would work, but it would cut the fighting force in half. This might prevent a decisive battle from being staged and prolong the attack indefinitely, the one thing they would want to avoid. We should be able to field about sixteen tanks ourselves, comes the big day, and twenty isn't enough of a margin over sixteen, even with our half-trained men. Brontke probably thinks this is the one we hope he'll do, so we can bet he won't.

'The second he may try, and it'll be up to us to prevent. The caches of fuel would have to be sneaked well inside of Jeppet territory, and we'll have to keep a sharp eye out for any attempt to do so and destroy the supplies before they can be built up. We're establishing a reconnaissance net over that three hundred miles of desert with every trick we know. We should be informed of every move the legion makes in this direction almost as soon as they make it.

'The third we'll have to watch out for, but I doubt if Brontke would be willing to use it. It would need a fifth column right in Akr itself. Even if such a thing existed, which I doubt, depending on its being able to sneak over eight tons of gasoline out of the city is a risk Brontke couldn't take.

'So we come to number four — using his own supply trucks.'

'I was wondering about that,' ben Dulli said. 'It seems to me the simplest and most sure. Just bring the trucks along right behind the tanks. The only way we could stop that would be to bomb the trucks, and he knows we can't do that.'

'True,' Tony said. 'And this is where our British colleague's photo recon again comes in valuable. Our analysis of the pictures tells us that the Desert Legion has about twenty-five trucks, and a little arithmetic leads us to the conclusion that they'd need only about twelve to fifteen of these to carry enough gas to do the job.'

'Your reasoning is fine,' Al-Rashid said, 'and up to now has been most heartening. You have led me to drink and then poisoned the water in my sight.'

Professor Perlemutter moved his bulk in the chair. 'The pill may prove bitter, but it's necessary to swallow, and we have the antidote,' he said.

Sheik Al-Rashid inclined his head toward the Professor. 'As always, you speak well. Please continue.'

Tony took up where he'd left off. 'The interesting thing about these trucks is their age. For most of them it's considerable. Whatever country supplied the tanks, it didn't come up to their quality with the auxiliary transport. I can pass on the assurance of our experts in these matters that not one truck in ten could make three hundred miles across open desert without breaking down. If we know this, it's a safe bet Brontke does, too.'

'Is this so?' ben Dulli demanded.

'It is,' Tony stated. 'Three hundred miles across the desert is quite a trip for heavily loaded trucks.'

'That means they couldn't count on getting more than three or four trucks across,' General Ashmed said.

'What you seem to have done,' ben Dulli said, 'is proved that the Desert Legion can't attack Jeppet. There must be a flaw in the reasoning.'

'What about the mountain highway?' the major asked. 'Couldn't they use that for trucks? It isn't quite the same thing as crossing open desert.' Peter put a star next to his mental resolve to make use of that major.

'Right,' Tony said. 'That's the flaw. The highway was built by the Allies during World War Two to ferry supplies from the Gulf north. It runs next to the mountains, and one point of it is less than thirty miles from Brontke's camp. Put the same trucks that would break down in open desert on three hundred miles of smooth concrete highway, and not more than three or four should break down, thus reversing the odds. Brontke can rendezvous his tanks with the trucks sixty to a hundred miles from here — the closer the better — and come on down the coast to sweep into Akr. The whole operation would cost him no more than sixty miles, about three hours' travel time, and however long it takes to fill his tanks.'

The general shrugged. 'That's it, then. That's how he'll beat us.'

Peter stood up. 'Kismet, General Ashmed? We haven't lost yet, and there's no reason why we should.'

'You have a scheme?' Al-Rashid asked.

'Professor Perlemutter has a scheme. I'll let him tell you about it.'

The Professor stood up and folded his hands across his stomach. 'Now,' he said, 'here's my plan . . . '

10

Commander-General Pertival Hals Von-und-Zu Brontke, late of Hitler's Wehrmacht, strode back and forth in front of his tent, his moustache twitching with anger. Lieutenant Khazar, standing in the formal 'at rest' position by the door of the tent, closed his eyes and mentally counted the steps. ' . . . six, seven, eight, nine, turn, one, two, three, four . . . This,' he reflected, 'could go on all night.'

Wake up!' a harsh, familiar voice grated in his ear. Lieutenant Khazar opened his eyes and found General Brontke's nose thrust three inches from his face. *Evil old man*, he thought, but he said, 'Yes, sir,' and kept his thoughts to himself.

'Go get Colonel Bahar.'

'Yes, sir.' Khazar saluted and dogtrotted off into the sand. General Brontke resumed his pacing.

The command tent, where Colonel Bahar was standing his turn as night duty officer, was clear across the area, but Lieutenant Khazar didn't even stop trotting when he was out of sight of the general. Brontke would have an exact idea of how long it would take and would be counting the seconds. 'You've been gone six minutes,' he would say when Khazar returned. 'It should have taken you four. Precision, I demand precision! Wasted time means inefficiency and lost battles. See that next time it only takes you four minutes.' And Khazar would have to stifle his reply that he'd like to see Brontke make it to the command tent and back in even six minutes and just say, 'Yes, sir.' It rankled. Sometimes he thought he'd been better off as a sergeant. He'd definitely had it better in the army he'd deserted from before he joined this bastard outfit. If only that captain had been away on maneuvers for two hours longer.

Khazar went through the double blackout flaps on the command tent and stood blinking in the sudden light. There was Bahar, asleep on the chair with his tunic open and his feet up on the desk. It was a good thing, Khazar reflected, that it was he who had come and not the general. 'Colonel Bahar,' he called softly. No response issued from the sleeping form. 'Colonel Bahar!' He approached the colonel, who was lightly snoring. He shook the colonel.

'Huh! Wha's wrong?' The colonel opened one eye slightly and peered through it. 'Oh, it's you, Khazar. What're you doing here? Here, have a drink.' He reached down and pulled a bottle up from the side of the desk. 'No cups; you'll have to drink it outta the bottle. It's okay though; no germs could live in this stuff,' he said, waving the bottle at Khazar.

'Oh crud!' Khazar said. 'Don't tell me you're drunk.'

'Won't breathe a word about it, if you don't,' Bahar promised.

'That won't do either of us any good,' Khazar yelped. 'The general wants to see you.'

'Nonshensh!' Bahar protested, losing his diction. 'Brontke's always in bed by ten if he doesn't have night duty. Told me so himself many times.'

Oho, Khazar thought. *Trouble*.

Bahar collapsed back in the chair. 'Come have a drink with me.'

'The general,' Khazar insisted, 'wants to see you right now. And you'd better get over there. He's pacing the ground.'

Bahar put the bottle down. 'Pacing? It must be pretty bad.'

'It's going to be a lot worse if he sees you like this.'

'Yesh. Yes. Yes, that's true.' Bahar shook himself. 'Instant sober, that's the ticket.' He got up and staggered to the back of the tent. Pulling a canvas water bucket from under a greasy tarpaulin, he staggered back with it and set it on the desk. 'One shec — second,' he announced. He rolled up his sleeves, folded his collar under, took a deep breath, and ducked his head into the bucket. Coming up, he said, 'Old family recipe; works every time,' took another breath and submerged again. This time he kept his head under the greasy water for so long that Khazar began to wonder if a man could drown in a bucket, but he finally came up. 'Feel better already,' he announced. 'Sober as a whatever. Toss me that shirt.' Khazar tossed him the khaki shirt that had been hanging over the back of a chair. Colonel Bahar dried himself off thoroughly with the shirt, ran a comb through his hair and rolled down his sleeves. 'Come on,' he said.

'Your tie!'

'Oh, right. Never do to let the general see me without a tie. I'd rather forget my pants.' He grabbed a brown uniform tie from the desk and started to adjust it as they left the tent.

Brontke was still pacing when they approached, and he didn't stop when he saw them. 'Twelve minutes,' he said in a petulant voice. 'Twelve whole minutes. Do you know what can happen in twelve minutes? We once beat the British because we were in position only five minutes before they were.'

Khazar hoped that he wouldn't tell the story, which he'd heard at least twenty times before. It would almost be better to get chewed out.

'It was the wireless,' Colonel Bahar improvised. 'I thought it might be one of our scouts calling in, but it was unclear. I had to wait till I could tell.'

Bahar, the lieutenant thought, had really done a splendid job of sobering up.

'What did the scout say?' Brontke asked, forgetting his anger. Scouts were instructed to maintain radio silence except for messages of prime importance.

'It turned out not to be a scout,' Bahar said. 'I think it was an American group on maneuvers somewhere. This desert will pull in radio waves from quite a distance sometimes.'

'On our frequency?' Brontke asked suspiciously.

Bahar shrugged. 'What can you expect if you're going to use surplus American equipment?' he asked. The drinking, Khazar decided, must really have given the rabbit courage for him to talk back to Brontke even that much.

Brontke, whose strong point was not the operation of radio equipment, nodded wisely. 'I see,' he said. He stopped pacing face to face with Bahar, who took a nervous step backward. 'Captain what's-his-name, any word from Captain what's-his-name?'

'Thor,' Bahar said. 'Captain Thor. No, no word from him.'

'We must find out what happened to him,' Brontke said. 'He's been gone for two days now with no sign.' He started to pace again.

'He must have deserted.' Bahar shrugged. 'I don't think he was ever very happy here. We have other men who can fly the plane.'

'That's not the point,' Brontke snapped. 'You're supposed to be my second-in-command, and you can't even see the point.' He marched up to Bahar and stuck his nose two inches away from his face. Bahar started to step back and then decided he'd better not. He stiffened. 'The truck,' Brontke said, 'is the point.'

'But we found it on the trail two days ago,' Bahar protested.

'That's just it,' Brontke said. 'If you were going to desert in the middle of a desert, would you leave your only means of transportation behind? With the truck he could have gotten somewhere; without it he'd walk until he died of thirst. And we know there haven't been any other vehicles on that trail. Besides, what happened to the driver?'

'Maybe el Quarat did away with both of them when they didn't find the machine guns in the shipment.'

'No,' Brontke said. 'That would be stupid. It would just ensure that they wouldn't get the guns in a later shipment. They aren't stupid.'

'Then what did happen to him?' Bahar asked.

'That, you dolt, is what has me worried. I'm even beginning to take half-seriously those stories about the Old Man of the Mountain.'

'I think that must be a myth, sir. A fairy story.'

'It wasn't for three centuries during the Middle Ages,' Brontke insisted. 'Why should it be now?'

'If you say so, sir,' Bahar said.

'Bah!' Brontke spat on the ground. 'If you disagree with me, say so!'

Bahar lost his temper for a second. 'I disagree with you? Of course I disagree with you; it's idiocy!'

It's alcohol, Khazar thought.

'How dare you?' Brontke shouted. 'You low-living, brainless, drunken — '

General Brontke never got a chance to finish. At that moment a dull, crumping explosion thudded through the air, followed by several lesser ones.

'A tank!' Brontke yelped. 'I'd know that sound anywhere. First the gas goes, then the ammunition.' He raced into his tent, and then ran out again, buckling on a gunbelt. 'Follow me,' he yelled.

The three of them raced through the night: Brontke in a series of gazelle-like leaps that outdistanced the younger men, Khazar in an easy lope, and Colonel Bahar in a puffing run. After what seemed only a few brief seconds, another, sharper crump sound. This time, perhaps because they were closer, they could feel the earth shake slightly.

'This way,' Brontke yelled, and they turned slightly and kept running. Suddenly flames erupted a good distance ahead of them, After a few seconds the flames spread, and the silhouette of a tank flickered against the black.

A machine gun sounded from in front of them; then, from the right, another. 'Our guards,' Brontke yelled exultantly.

'It's about time.'

As they reached the flickering tank, a guard ran around from its other side waving a machine gun. He steadied and took aim at them.

'Sea Lion!' Khazar yelled, remembering the password for the day. 'For the love of God, Sea Lion!' The guard lowered his gun and squinted into the dark. When he saw who it was, he stiffened to attention, and presented his arms.

'What happened?' Brontke yelled.

'I'm not sure, sir,' the guard said. 'All I know is he got the tank, then I got him.'

'Where is he?' Brontke demanded, coming to a stop in front of the guard. Khazar joined him, and Bahar sat down in the sand behind them, panting.

'On the other side of the tank, sir.'

'Very good,' Brontke said. 'Check and see if there are any more.'

'Yes, sir.' The guard raised his gun to an even stiffer present-arms position, then went off at a dead run.

'Well,' Brontke said, rounding on the tank. 'Well, well.' A little man wearing nothing but a loincloth was curled up in the sand. He looked as though he was asleep, with his eyes closed peacefully, but there were at least six bullet holes in his head and chest, and the blood was still welling out of them to be sopped up by the sand. Khazar fought down an impulse to be sick.

'There were more shots over that way,' General Brontke said. 'Let's see about them. Bahar, we should . . . Bahar? Bahar!'

'Here, sir,' Colonel Bahar said, puffing around the tank.

'You're out of shape, Colonel. Out of shape.' Brontke chuckled, which brought back memories of a tiger clearing its throat. 'So's he,' he added, kicking the corpse. He broke into a trot, and this time Colonel Bahar stayed right behind, letting Khazar bring up the rear.

Their way was illuminated by another blazing tank, and this time the guard standing by it recognized them before he started waving his gun around.

'Report,' Brontke barked.

'Yes, sir. I was making my rounds as usual when I heard a noise from that direction.' He indicated the way they had come. 'Before I could do anything about it, that there tank blew up. Then, when I started running that way, this here tank blew up. I ran back just in time to see some Gingo making it away, so I let him have it with a burst from my gun. He fell down and started to crawl away, so I gave him another.'

'Unwise,' Brontke said. 'You should have captured him. But I guess in the excitement of the moment you did as well as could be expected. Where is he?'

The guard pointed to the foot of the blazing tank, and they could just make out a huddled figure. 'Let's have a look,' Brontke said, and they went over to the body. Ignoring the heat of the blazing tank, which kept the other two a short distance away, Brontke bent over the prostrate form. 'They could be brothers,' he said, pushing the body over on its back.

'He's smiling,' Khazar said, forgetting to be sick.

'He has reason to be pleased,' Brontke said sourly. 'Two tanks gone.'

'Must be fifteen bullet holes in him,' Khazar persisted, 'and he's smiling.'

'I'd say,' Brontke commented, getting up and dusting his trousers off, 'that this — person — was very sure of where he was going from this sphere of existence.'

'What's that?' Bahar yelped, as something rolled out of the dead man's hand.

'A bottle,' Brontke said. He bent over to look closer, then stood up and backed away quickly. 'A Molotov cocktail. Saw them at Stalingrad. Bottle full of gas with a cotton wick. Light wick; bash over tank; gas seeps in and burns. Incinerates crew; sets off explosives. Very nasty. Uncivilized. The gas is leaking out of this one. We'd better get away.'

The three of them backed off, watching the body lying on the oil-soaked sand with a morbid fascination. Suddenly a white haze seemed to flicker over the area, and a sheet of flame enveloped the corpse, licking hungrily at the thin body. The smile, it seemed to Khazar, was the only recognizable feature. He was sick.

11

Lieutenant Akrat sat ill at ease on the edge of his chair across the breakfast table from Peter and Professor Perlemutter. 'I wish I could be of more help to you,' he said, 'but you must remember I was rather young when I was separated from the tribe.'

'It's social mores we're most interested in,' Professor Perlemutter said, cracking open the top of his soft-boiled egg, 'and that sort of thing you'd know as a mere baby without being particularly aware of it. It would just seem to be the way you live.'

'What do you mean?' asked Akrat.

'Well, for example: when we drive in, should we be unarmed?'

'No,' Lieutenant Akrat said. 'Definitely not. Among others it might be a sign that you come in friendship, but with el Quarat, you're less than a man if you don't carry a gun. It would be best, however, to wear it slung over your back and not carry it in your hand. That might be regarded as hostile.'

'I see,' Perlemutter said. 'That's what I mean. The kind of thing that you'd regard as natural, but we have to be told.'

'Now I understand what you mean,' Akrat said. He brooded for a minute over his scrambled eggs. 'I'd suggest you don't wear uniforms. Quarati don't trust uniforms.'

Peter looked down at his loose-fitting khaki shirt and army-style khaki pants. 'I guess these do look rather like a uniform,' he admitted.

'No,' Lieutenant Akrat said, inspecting him, 'that'll do. It's recognized as standard dress for the non-Arab, and the fact that you and the Professor are dressed alike won't matter. As long as there are no patches or other insignia on your clothes.'

'Right,' Peter agreed. 'No patches.'

'I can't think of anything else,' Akrat said.

Peter asked, 'What kind of reception can we expect when we get there?'

'I can't predict. They'll either shoot you on sight or Mondar will break bread with you. If that happens, you're his guest, and completely safe.'

'Completely?' the Professor asked.

'Yes. It's a point of honor. The position of host implies responsibilities. Once a rebellion against the Turks was held up for four days because the local Turkish commander happened to come through on a tour and was put up in the home of the Sheik leading the rebellion.'

'Sounds convincing,' Peter admitted. 'We'll look forward to Mondar's hospitality.'

'I wish I could go with you,' Akrat said, 'since I know the customs. But I don't think my presence would aid the cause.'

'That's unfortunate,' Professor Perlemutter said, 'but true. However, the assistance you have given us this morning may prove of some use, and I thank you.' He pushed himself away from the remains of his breakfast. 'We had best be going.'

The Land Rover that was waiting for them in the courtyard was fitted out for desert travel, with great splay tires, canvas top and water bags hanging from the side. In the back were their bags and a radio, the long whip antenna of which rose from the rear of the vehicle.

Peter turned the radio on and checked its setting. Then he picked up the microphone. 'Teakettle, this is Sand Flea,' he called. 'Can you hear me?'

'Sand Flea,' Tony Ryan's voice came back over the set, 'this is Teakettle. You're coming in nine-by-nine. It's like you're right below me.'

'What hath God wrought?' Peter said into the mike, then signed off. He looked at one of the upstairs windows of the palace and saw Tony waving at him.

'You may proceed with this caravan,' Professor Perlemutter announced, settling himself comfortably into the passenger's seat.

'Very good, Herr Doktor Professor,' Peter said, swinging himself into the driver's seat. He started the car and drove through the gate onto the desert road.

The early-morning sun was behind them as they went; the desert was still cool from the previous night, and they made good time. The ornate walls of the palace dwindled behind them, merging with the glitter of the sun, and soon all trace of the works of man save the road itself had disappeared. They rode on steadily, but the mountains in front of them seemed to stay the same distance away.

The only sounds were the growl of the engine and the hum of the wind, and it quickly grew hotter. 'How long,' Professor Perlemutter asked, taking his wide-brimmed hat off and wiping his neck, 'have we been going?'

'About three hours,' Peter said, glancing at his watch.

'Ah,' Perlemutter said, 'and how far have we come?'

'About a hundred and ten miles.'

'Ah,' the Professor said again. 'It seems like longer and farther. I can see that it's easy to lose track of time and distance in the desert.' By now the sun was directly overhead, and the heat rose in glittering waves off the highway in front of them.

Professor Perlemutter pulled one of the water bags in from the side of the car, took a deep drink, and offered it to Peter. He took it, wet his lips and handed it back. 'Ah, yes,' Perlemutter said, fastening the bag back where it belonged. 'Water control. Don't drink too much in the desert heat; it isn't good for you. I've heard the theory, of course, and I don't doubt it. But my willpower is always so sadly lacking. It's unbelievably hot out here.'

'It'll be cool tonight,' Peter said, 'and we should be there by this time tomorrow.'

'It'll be cold tonight,' Perlemutter corrected. 'The desert is a place of great contrast in climate, if nothing else.'

They rode on for a while in silence, the Professor taking a book on chess end games out of his pocket and reading it diligently, pausing only to mop his neck or forehead.

'Look,' Peter said, pulling the Professor's attention from a tricky knight mate. 'We are not alone.'

The Professor peered out of the windshield and could make out a black dot moving in the distance. 'What do you suppose it is?'

'A ship of the desert,' Peter said. 'And,

unless I'm mistaken, all alone.'

'A camel?' the Professor asked. 'Who'd be out here all by himself? I thought camels usually traveled in large caravans.'

'So did I,' Peter said. 'But we'll find out soon enough. It's headed this way.'

After another five minutes they were close enough to see that it was indeed all alone striding purposefully through the desert without rider or driver. They pulled up to it and stopped. 'Here's a mystery,' Peter said, going over to the beast, which didn't shy away and even seemed glad to see him. 'It's got a saddle on, but no pack.'

'It must have broken away from someone,' Professor Perlemutter ventured. 'Probably during the night when they were bedded out, since it's carrying no pack.'

'Good logic,' Peter said. 'The question now is, what are we going to do with it?'

'We certainly can't take it with us,' Perlemutter agreed, walking over to take a closer look at the animal. 'I'll offer two more observations: it broke away recently, probably last night, as it hasn't divested itself of the saddle yet; and its rider was an amateur, both because he went to bed without taking the camel's saddle off and because he tethered it so poorly that it was able to get away.'

'Sounds right,' Peter said. He loosened the animal's harness and removed it, laying it on the side of the road. 'We'll have to let it go on, but this should help. It seems to know the way.'

'I should think it will make out all right. I'll just give it some water,' said Professor Perlemutter. He got out a canvas bucket and filled it partway from one of the water bags. When the bucket was held out to the beast, it emptied it quickly and noisily.

'By popular legend it should be good for a month on that water,' Peter said.

'I should think five days would be more like it, and by then it'll be pretty thirsty. But it should make Akr by then.'

'I'll tell them to expect it, tonight when I call in,' Peter said, climbing back into the car. 'We'd better be going.'

'Yes,' the Professor agreed. He fitted the bucket back into its niche and returned to his seat.

The car started off, and the camel stared sorrowfully at its retreating shape for a while, then resumed its journey home. They stopped for a quick lunch after a while and then resumed the trip, the Professor taking his turn driving. He drove well but with a sort of precision that was alien to American drivers. He didn't seem to have the feel of the gears but shifted with an exact motion according to the dictates of a little red line on the speedometer. He handled the wheel as though it were a large water faucet.

After they had driven a while farther, Perlemutter tapped Peter on the shoulder. 'What's our policy in regard to hitch-hikers?'

Peter looked up. The ball of the sun was poised on the tips of the mountains before them, and under it, framed by the long rays that wavered through the baked air, was a sight that gave new life to the word incongruous.

A woman had stepped out of the pages of a fashion magazine and was standing by the side of the road. Her jacket was white; her skirt, modestly a bit longer than a miniskirt, was white; her legs were long, golden brown, terminating in light brown sandals; and her hair, a glorious blonde, cascaded over her shoulders almost to her waist. She had one foot on a long, round, white canvas bag, and her hand was raised in the universal gesture of the hitchhiker. Her knees, Peter noticed with a rising sense of disbelief, were slightly knobby.

'I think we'd better stop,' Professor Perlemutter suggested.

'What?' Peter said. 'Oh, yes. Yes, we'd better stop.'

The Land Rover pulled over to the side of the road where the woman was standing, and Professor Perlemutter stuck his head out of the window. 'We can, maybe, be of some assistance to you?' he asked formally.

'It's about time somebody got here,' the woman said. 'I'm glad to see you. I've been waiting here all day, and you're the first ones to pass.' She picked up her bag and attempted to put it in the back of the car, but it was too much for her and fell out of her hands. Then her reserve strength broke, and she collapsed on top of the bag and started crying softly.

Peter got out of the car and went around to the woman. 'Let me help you,' he said. He opened the rear door, cleared away luggage to make space for her and her bag, then tossed the bag in and helped her in gently. She tried to smile at him but broke into tears again. Peter closed the door and went around to his own side and climbed in. Perlemutter started the car again with a methodical meshing of gears, and they were off.

Peter pulled a handkerchief out of his pocket and passed it back to the woman. 'Here, dry your eyes.'

'Thank you,' she said, taking the offered cloth. She patted her hair lightly and then wiped her face. 'I must look a mess,' she said, starting to dig into the pocket of the bag by her side.

'Not at all,' Peter said honestly.

'Could it,' Professor Perlemutter asked, keeping his eye on the road, 'have been your camel we passed earlier today?'

'Yes,' the woman said. 'I hobbled him

when I went to sleep last night, but when I woke up he'd gone. I fancy I did it improperly.' She said it very seriously, but then started crying again.

'It's all right,' Peter assured her. 'We've found you, and there's no harm done.'

'That's true,' she said. 'I'm so glad you came along. It's just my own blasted incompetence. I had always thought I was so capable, and now this.'

Peter noticed that she spoke with some sort of British accent, which he found charming. She fished around in the pocket of the suitcase until she came up with a small mirror, and then examined her face critically. It, Peter observed, was a fine face. 'You're British,' he said, mainly to make conversation.

'Yes,' the woman admitted.

'What on earth are you doing out here?'

She finally managed a small smile. 'Well, I suppose it's going to sound horribly melodramatic or something, but I'm hunting for my brother.'

'In the middle of the desert?'

'Not exactly. You see, he's disappeared, and they think he's been captured by

some native tribe, so I'm going to see.'
She stated it as though it were the most
natural thing in the world.

'Oh,' Peter said, 'of course.'

'I know it's dreadfully silly. At least I
know that now, but it seemed perfectly
logical back in Akr. Nobody wanted to let
me go, of course, but they couldn't really
stop me. And, you see, I have to know
what happened to him.'

'You,' Peter said, announcing his great
revelation, 'must be Alan Quinline's sister.'

'That's right,' the woman said. 'So you
know about it. My name is Sara Quinline.
Alan is six years older than me, and there's
no more family, so we're very close.'

'It was still very silly to come out in the
desert after him alone, Miss Quinline,'
Professor Perlemutter scolded from the
vantage point of his middle age and
advanced corpulence.

'You're probably right,' Sara admitted,
'Mister, uh . . .'

'Oh,' Peter said. 'I'm sorry. This is
Professor Perlemutter, and my name
is Peter Carthage.'

'You're probably right, Professor. But

I'm going to go on.' She sounded very stubborn. 'Why are you here? Some sort of archaeological expedition?'

'Not exactly,' Peter told her. 'As a matter of fact, we're going to visit el Quarat, the tribe that might have captured your brother.'

'Oh!' Sara exclaimed. 'Will you take me with you? Please?'

'Well,' Peter said, thinking out loud, 'there's no place between here and there to drop you off, and we haven't time to turn back, so we'll take you.'

'Thank you. I do appreciate it very much.'

'But there are a few ground rules,' Peter told her.

'Of what sort?'

'The mission we're on is very important, and the Quarati believe that a woman's place is at the rear of the tent, not asking questions. So you'll have to agree to stay very much in the background. In return we'll find out what we can about your brother and try to get his release if he is their captive.'

'I'll agree,' Sara said, 'gladly. But what do you mean, 'if he is their captive'? He has to be; where else could he be?'

'There are problems with that point of view,' Peter said, thinking of what Lieutenant Akrat had said about the separate camels bearing Quinline off, 'but you're probably right.'

The last rays of the sun disappeared behind the mountain, and a sudden chill swept across the newly dark desert. The stars started to appear, and in a few minutes it was pitch black. 'We might as well stop here as anywhere,' Peter said. 'I have to call in a minute.'

'Okay,' Professor Perlemutter said, steering the car off the road onto the sand. 'We stop here.' He switched off the engine, and the sudden absolute silence hit them an almost physical blow.

'I'll do something about dinner,' the Professor offered, 'and you play with your radio.'

'Dinner,' Sara said. 'It sounds wonderful. I'd forgotten all about food.'

'Only sandwiches, I'm afraid,' Perlemutter apologized, 'but we'll have hot coffee.'

'That's quite all right,' she assured him.

'Although in the novels everyone dresses for dinner and they have five courses and three sorts of wine.'

'Those are nineteenth-century English romances,' Peter told her.

'I read quite a lot of nineteenth-century English romances.'

'I can tell,' Peter said. He climbed in back and dug the obstructions from in front of the radio.

Sara stalked over to where Professor Perlemutter was setting up a canned heat burner for the coffee. 'Whatever did he mean by that?'

'It wasn't an insult,' the Professor assured her. Peter turned the radio on to 'receive.'

'Teakettle calling Sand Flea. Teakettle calling Sand Flea. Over.'

Peter pushed the talk button on the microphone. 'Sand Flea calling Teakettle. How are you receiving me?'

'Nine-by-nine,' Tony answered from the palace station. 'This desert is great for radio waves. Turn your volume down.'

Peter twisted the volume knob slightly. 'Better?'

'Much,' Tony said. 'We anxiously await your report. Have you seen anything besides sand?'

'I have,' Peter said, remembering his first view of Sara Quinline. He reported the day's events in detail. When he was finished, and the radio was back on receive, he could hear Tony laughing. Also, he suspected, some more people in the background.

'Quite a story,' Tony said, still chuckling.

'Who's there with you?' Peter asked.

'Eric and most of the rest of the group. We've all got together and we agree. For sheer undeserved luck, nothing can top a Carthage.' He then proceeded to tell Peter what they had decided he could fall into and still come up smelling like various assorted flowers. 'And there you are,' he finished, 'just you and her. Surrounded by hundreds of miles of desert. Ah, romance. Ah, desert moonlight. Ah, Carthage, sometimes you make me sick.'

'There's no moon,' Peter reminded him, 'and we're chaperoned.'

'I'm sure you can work out something

161

with the good Professor,' Tony chuckled. 'And with your luck, a moon will be provided.'

Peter, for some unaccountable reason, was starting to get angry with the banter. 'Is that all?' he asked.

'I'm afraid so,' Tony said. 'Nothing new at this end. Good luck.' He chuckled again. 'Sleep well.'

'Right,' Peter said. 'Out.'

'Out,' Tony agreed, and the radio was silent. Peter turned it off and climbed out of the car.

'Come have your coffee,' Perlemutter called, and Peter went over to sit on the sand and receive his steaming mug.

'It's cold,' Sara said, huddling up next to Peter.

'Have you a jacket?' Peter asked.

'Yes, but I've such a sunburn that it would hurt to put it on.'

'I'm not surprised. You weren't exactly dressed for desert travel.'

'That's right, my dear,' Professor Perlemutter said in his most fatherly, or perhaps Dutch uncle, tone. 'This sun needs shielding from as much as the cold.'

'I've learned my lesson,' Sara said. 'I'll dress more sensibly tomorrow.'

'I'll get you something for the sunburn,' said Peter, who was sorry to hear of the sensible dress. He went back to the car, and emerged from it a minute later with a tube of ointment. 'Here, I'll rub it in for you.'

'Thank you,' Sara said, presenting her back to him.

He rubbed the ointment into her back and shoulders, gently massaging the firm skin beneath his hand. He found himself thinking of another woman on other sand, where the ocean waves applauded the beach and a crackling fire kept away the night air and the insects. But that, he reminded himself, was long ago and far away; besides, the lady had not been hunting for her missing brother. 'Here,' he said, handing her the tube, 'you'd better do your legs.'

Sara looked at him in the dark — or perhaps it was through him. 'Yes, I think I'd better.'

'It's time to think about going to bed,' Professor Perlemutter said, carefully collecting the empty cups. 'Have you a sleeping bag, Miss Quinline?'

'Sara,' she said. 'Call me Sara. Yes, I have one, but I'll need help getting it. I forgot to bring a flashlight.'

'Come along with me then,' Peter said. He guided her back to the car and held his flashlight for her while she unzipped one side of her valise and extracted a sleeping bag.

'Clever luggage,' Peter commented.

'Yes,' she said, 'I thought so. At least I didn't do everything wrong.'

'I think you've done pretty well,' Peter said. He pulled out a pair of sleeping bags from the back and toted them to the camp. He tossed one to the Professor and spread open his own on the ground. The Professor opened his methodically, tugging at corners and spreading the canvas carefully underneath. Sara unrolled hers between them. Peter could hear her undressing, and then she slid into the sleeping bag without bothering to unzip the side.

Professor Perlemutter took off his shoes and placed them carefully at the foot of his sleeping bag. He then removed his outer garments, folded them neatly, and put them by his shoes. 'Good night,' he said, unzipping his sleeping bag and rolling into it.

'Good night,' Sara said softly.

'Good night,' Peter echoed. He finished the cigarette he was smoking, tossed it away, and then took off his shoes and crawled into his own sleeping bag. For a few minutes he stared at the stars, then he was asleep.

★　★　★

Sometime after midnight, Peter woke up. At first he thought it was morning; then he realized that the moon had risen low on the horizon, and its clean glare was lighting up the desert. For some reason he didn't understand, this struck him as funny. Then he remembered what Tony had said about a moon being provided. He rolled over to look at Sara. Her slim face, framed by golden hair, stuck out of the top of her sleeping bag, looking unbelievably sweet and innocent. Her perfume was carried over to Peter by the desert air, and it smelled of flowers and promises. Peter looked at her for a long while; then he sighed and rolled over, going back to sleep. His dreams were good.

The next morning when Peter awoke, Sara was already up and dressed. She was scrubbed and bright, and her garb, as promised, was a sensible long skirt and long-sleeved jacket. She was even wearing a cotton hat with a brim that clearly declared to all who saw it, 'deserts — for use in.' The loose garb reduced her apparent age from twenty-plus to somewhere in the early teens, and Peter felt a faint regret. He slid out of his own sleeping bag, and she, with a sense of propriety Peter felt he should admire but couldn't, turned around while he put his pants and shirt on.

'Good morning,' she said cheerfully. 'Breakfast's ready.' She brought him over a cup of coffee and a roll still wrapped in wax paper.

'Just the coffee,' Peter growled, accepting the cup from her outstretched hand. 'Thank you. Where's the Professor?'

'Well, you're certainly not at your best

in the morning,' Sara said. 'Professor Perlemutter is putting the things away in the car. Doesn't he have a first name? I can't keep calling him 'Professor Perlemutter.''

'I don't know myself,' Peter said. 'I'll ask.' He rolled up his sleeping bag and started back to the car. Professor Perlemutter was just finishing stowing the coffee pot. 'Professor,' Peter asked, tossing his bedroll in the rear of the vehicle, 'what's your first name?'

Perlemutter favored Peter with his approximation of an evil glare. 'Why this sudden interest in my name?' he demanded.

'It's not me. Sara doesn't feel right calling you 'Professor Perlemutter.''

'Is that right?' the Professor asked, transferring the glare to Sara.

'It's just that it seems so unfriendly calling you by your last name all the time. I mean, I want you to call me Sara, and not Miss Quinline, and I want to call Peter by his first name and you by yours.'

'It's Sigismund,' announced the Professor reluctantly. 'I was named after my grandfather.'

Sara clapped. 'I can call you Ziggie,' she said.

'You do,' Perlemutter said grimly, 'and one of us will walk.'

'But, Ziggie,' she protested, 'you wouldn't make me walk, dear Ziggie, would you?'

The Professor glowered.

12

The point where the mountain trail reached the road was not exactly hidden, just sort of unadvertised. They found the entrance to the trail easily, but only because Lieutenant Akrat had described it well. The trail, as Akrat had said, was quite passable to a car driving carefully. Slowly the mountains grew up around them until there were steep cliffs on both sides of the car. Then all at once the cliffs broke away, and they entered a small valley.

Five horsemen rose from nowhere and barred their way. The men sat casually, and their faces were impassive, but each had a rifle, and each rifle pointed steadily at the car.

'Very impressive, that,' Professor Perlemutter said as Peter braked to a stop.

'Very,' Peter agreed. He got out of the car slowly, his rifle, as Akrat had directed, strapped to his back, his hands empty. 'You are Quarati,' he said, facing the riders. The men stared at him. 'We would like to see your leader,' Peter called out. The men kept staring at him.

Sara leaned forward from the back seat. 'You don't speak Arabic?' she asked softly.

'Their boss speaks English,' Peter told her. 'Went to school in England.'

'That doesn't help with his men,' Sara said. 'Let me.' She got out of the car and, staying directly behind Peter with her head down, mumbled something to the men. One of them barked a sharp question to her, and she replied in the same mumble. Without another word, the five horsemen turned around and started riding off slowly.

'Follow them,' Sara said, climbing back into the car.

Peter got back in, started the engine, and joined the procession. 'What did you say to them?' he asked.

'I was very respectful,' she said, 'as they expect from a woman. I told them that my master wanted to see their chief.'

'What did they ask you?'

'Why my master couldn't speak their language.'

'And you said?'

'That he's never deigned to tell me, and I wouldn't dare ask. They liked that.'

'Very good,' Professor Perlemutter said joyously. 'Excellent. I couldn't have done better myself.'

Sara smiled. 'Thank you, Ziggie.'

Perlemutter ignored her. 'I can see,' he mused, 'why this place has never been attacked. Five men on those cliffs we passed could hold off an armored regiment. If there's no other entrance to this valley, the place is impregnable.'

'I doubt that there's another entrance,' Peter said. 'I'm surprised that during el Quarat's periodic trips north someone else doesn't move into the valley and hold it against them.'

'That's simple,' the Professor said. 'There isn't enough water here to grow any crop on a regular basis. This place is great for a nomadic tribe but worthless to anyone else.'

As they drove on, more riders appeared, flanking the car on both sides and bringing up the rear. It was an impressive procession, if slightly frightening to be in the middle of.

'Are they going to take us to their camp?' Sara asked. 'Or are they just leading us somewhere to shoot us?'

'Your guess is better than mine,' Professor Perlemutter said. 'You spoke to them.'

'They're taking us to their camp,' Peter said.

'How can you be so sure?' asked Professor Perlemutter.

'Easy,' Peter said. 'Here's their camp.' A large circle of white tents had just come into view in front of them.

Sara leaned forward. 'Don't introduce me,' she whispered to Peter. 'It isn't done.' Peter nodded.

The procession entered the camp and stopped. The group of horsemen fell aside, forming two rows. At the end of the lane thus created stood a tall man with a large angular nose. His chin was prominent, and it supported a neat triangular beard. His arms were folded and his bearing was proud. He reminded Peter of a stern father about to speak to his errant children.

'You wished to see me?'

Peter and the Professor got out of the car and stood facing this man. 'You are Sherif of el Quarat?' Peter asked.

'I am Mondar,' the man stated. 'First among equals. You may speak with me.'

Looking at the fierce, proud riders that surrounded him, Peter understood the title. 'I am Peter Carthage. My companion is Professor Sigismund Perlemutter.'

The Professor winced. 'We come in peace to speak with you.' As instructed, Peter didn't introduce Sara. It seemed right, as Mondar nodded and didn't ask.

'Carthage,' the Sherif said. 'Perlemutter.' He repeated the unfamiliar syllables a few times to get his tongue used to them. 'What have we to speak about?'

Peter had a speech prepared, but for some reason he couldn't think of it. 'We have been to Akr,' he said, 'and spoken with the Sheik. Now we come to speak with you. It is on a matter that concerns you both.'

Mondar took a step toward them. 'You speak for the Sheik of Jeppet?' he asked, sounding angry.

'No,' Peter said, matching him in anger

and hoping that this was the right note. 'We speak for ourselves.'

Mondar appeared satisfied. 'It is good. Come, we will lunch together and speak afterward.' He said something to his men, and they dispersed, some dismounting and leading their horses away, and some riding madly off. Mondar turned and started walking toward a large tent that was slightly set off from the others. Peter and the Professor followed. Peter was wondering what to do with Sara, and he was relieved to see a slim woman, the first he had seen in the camp, run out to the car. She spoke briefly with Sara, and the two went off together.

Mondar waited for them by the entrance of the tent. 'You may leave your arms outside,' he said. 'It is the custom.'

Peter, glad to be relieved of the weight of what was purely a symbol in this camp of armed men, unstrapped his rifle and leaned it against the wall of the tent. Professor Perlemutter followed suit.

'It is a good weapon,' Mondar said, looking at Peter's rifle. 'May I see it?'

Peter picked up the gun and handed it

to Mondar. It was a finely engraved Winchester Model 98 lever-action thirty-caliber, with a low serial number. 'It was my father's,' Peter said, 'and his father's.'

This was true. Professor Perlemutter was carrying an army carbine; but Peter, who had brought the gun to Jeppet, thinking he might have time for hunting whatever the area considered big game, considered the old Winchester a better symbol. His grandfather had proved his manhood with it and fed and defended a family.

Mondar squinted down the length of the octagonal barrel through the rear notch sight, flipped the front sight from bar to peep several times, and felt the weight of the weapon in his hands.

'It is good,' he decided, handing the rifle back to Peter, who put it down.

'It is,' Peter agreed.

Mondar reached inside the tent, and from the doorway produced an ancient long-barreled rifle. 'My father's,' he said, handing it to Peter, 'and his before him.'

Peter hefted the weapon, which was exceedingly heavy. The gold inlay work on the barrel and stock had grown smooth from years of handling, but its delicate tracings were still quite clear. It had originally been a flintlock, Peter noted, but at some time over the years had been converted to cap and ball. Peter passed it to Professor Perlemutter, who examined it silently and then handed it back to Peter, pointing to an inscription on the barrel. There, quite faded but still easy to read, was the name and time of the maker: 'Wm Morrison & Son. Fine Gunsmythes Edinburgh, Scotland 1812.'

Peter handed the gun gingerly back to Mondar. 'It's beautiful,' he said. 'It must have quite a history behind it.'

'It is possessed of a fine history,' Mondar assured them. He put the gun back in its place and led the way inside the tent. There, Peter found, it was dark but cool. The direct rays of the sun were shut out, and from somewhere a slight breeze blew through the room.

When his eyes had adjusted to the lack of light and he could make out the details of the room, Peter was awed. Professor Perlemutter went over to examine the details of the drapery that surrounded them, but Peter just stood in the center of the room, getting the total effect of the rich masses of color. It seemed that new bits of design were constantly being revealed to him as the light in the huge tent subtly changed.

'You like my walls?' Mondar asked.

'These hangings,' Perlemutter told him, 'would grace the palace of any king.'

Mondar smiled. 'So I think also,' he said. 'Come, let us sit down and break bread together.'

They sat cross-legged on cushions around a large, low table. Mondar clapped his hands, and a woman — Peter thought it was the same one he had seen before — came in and knelt before him, bearing white linen towels in her outstretched hands. Mondar took one, and the ceremony was repeated before Peter and the Professor. The towels, Peter found, were not for use as napkins but were damp, almost wet. Mondar used his to wipe his hands and face, then tossed it into a silver tray at one side. Peter and Professor Perlemutter did likewise, and Peter decided it was an excellent custom.

Next, beaten silver plates were brought in and passed out, each containing a large flat roll. Then a large silver platter was placed on the table. The platter was filled with what proved to be a mixture of lamb and rice, along with several ingredients Peter couldn't identify. A samovar stood at the side of the mat, and tea was poured into small handle-less cups and given out. There was no silverware.

The method of eating, Peter discovered by letting the Sherif start, was to take up the bread, break off a large piece, and by using that and your right hand as a shovel, transfer the food from the platter to your plate and thence to your mouth. It proved to be less messy than Peter expected, since the consistency of the rice and lamb dish made it stick together quite nicely in little balls. It was, Peter decided after he'd somewhat gotten used to it, all quite good.

'Tell me about yourselves,' Mondar said, gesturing with a lump of lamb.

Peter decided that he meant background, not business, and he and Professor Perlemutter took turns telling

Mondar about the function and purpose of War, Inc. Mondar watched them intently while they talked, his only motions being the lifting of food to his mouth and the up-and-down bobbing of his chin while he chewed. He evidently heard and understood every word they said, for his questions were intelligent and perceptive.

'You speak English well,' Peter complimented him at one point in the conversation.

'I was sent to school in England when I was nine years old,' Mondar said. 'I stayed there until my father died when I was fifteen, and I had to come back. I did not like it.'

After the meal, towels were handed around again — this time they were hot — and the plates were removed. 'Now we talk,' Mondar said.

As if it were a cue, and perhaps it was, an older man with a distinguished length of white beard parted one of the curtains and came over to sit beside Mondar. 'Ben Sinna,' Mondar introduced. 'My adviser. He doesn't speak English too well, although he understands it, so he'll just sit by me and listen.' The man nodded his head deeply to the two visitors. Mondar sat back on a cushion with his legs crossed, his body relaxed and his eyes intent. 'What have I to do with the Sheik of Jeppet?' he asked.

Peter decided that if the cross-legged position were an endurance contest, Mondar would win; he himself was already stiff. 'I explained to you the function of my company,' he said.

Mondar nodded. 'Yes.'

'Well, we're now on a training mission in Jeppet.'

'So I had assumed. You are teaching them to fight against my people.'

'No, the danger to Jeppet is not from el Quarat.' This was the delicate part. 'For ages you have raided the lowlands in the countries you travel through, but only for what you need to live.

You have been fierce warriors but never senseless destroyers. But now you attack oil stations in the desert that can neither help nor harm you. You are doing someone's bidding, and this person is not a friend of el Quarat.'

Ben Sinna said something to Mondar in an urgent undertone, but the leader shook his head impatiently. 'Talk,' he said. 'Explain.'

It had been agreed beforehand that flat, direct honesty was their best course, and Peter hoped they were right. Professor Perlemutter took up where he'd left off. 'You know the Desert Legion?' the Professor asked.

'The collection of machines and men out in the sand,' Mondar said. 'We know them.'

'They give you weapons you could not otherwise get,' the Professor said. 'In return you commit acts you would not otherwise do. They have promised you something. I do not know what it is, but I can tell you they will not keep their promise.'

'They promise only to leave us alone,' Mondar said.

'They lie,' Perlemutter insisted. 'That's the one promise they can't possibly keep.'

'Show me this,' Mondar said.

'For the first time in many hundreds of

years, Jeppet is again a rich country. This is because of the oil that has been found under its sand. The Desert Legion wishes to destroy Jeppet and take it over because of this oil. That is why this army sits out in the sand and waits for the British to leave.'

'So we had guessed,' Mondar said.

'Such a force,' said the Professor, 'doesn't spring up by itself. Such weapons are not obtained out of the air. The legion is supported by another country that desires to have these riches.'

Mondar leaned over and held a hurried consultation with his aide. Peter wished that he could understand Arabic. 'Interesting,' Mondar said, straightening up. 'Continue. What is this other country?'

'Since no nation admits its connection with this illegal army that is carefully hidden, I could guess, but that would profit us nothing. Nonetheless, there is — there must be — such a country.'

'It is logical,' Mondar admitted.

'Then let us look at the way this country does things. It is deceitful. It lies, since all countries have denied any connection with the legion. It uses force to get what it wants. The Desert Legion is an example of that force. Today you can help it. Someday, perhaps not tomorrow or even next year, you will be in its way. On that day it will smash you.'

'And what of Al-Rashid, the Sheik of Jeppet — would he not also smash us if he could?'

'The Sheik is not power hungry. They have found oil in Jeppet, and this is good. The money will enable him to do things for his people. He is building roads, schools and hospitals. Within two years he hopes to have every child in Jeppet in school.'

Mondar nodded. 'School is good. But what has this to do with el Quarat?'

'The Sheik,' Professor Perlemutter told him, 'would consider you among his people.'

'We are no one's people,' Mondar said softly.

'Not his subjects,' Professor Perlemutter said. 'His people. The people of Jeppet, who should share in the good fortune of the oil riches. He would build schools for your children.'

'This,' Mondar said, 'which sounds so good, would mean an end to our way of life.'

Professor Perlemutter took a deep breath. 'Look around you outside of this valley,' he said. 'Your way of life is fast coming to an end.'

Ben Sinna yelled something in Arabic and sprang to his feet. Mondar jumped up and replied in as loud a tone. The two of them, yelling and gesticulating, strode out of the tent, leaving Peter and the Professor sitting there.

'Something got to them,' Peter said.

Professor Perlemutter agreed. 'They looked angry,' he said mildly. 'For a second I thought they were going to get to us.'

'It's quite a shock to be suddenly told that your way of life is obsolete,' said Peter.

'That it is,' Perlemutter said. 'I think our only hope is the seven years Mondar spent in a British public school he didn't like.'

Mondar and ben Sinna stalked back in

and sat down. 'I apologize for our rudeness,' Mondar said. 'Whatever our feelings, we should listen to what guests have to say and think carefully on their words and on our reply.' He glared at ben Sinna, who glared back.

'I, in turn, apologize for having offended you,' the Professor said. 'But right or wrong, it is my obligation to speak what I believe to be the truth.'

Mondar stared at him for a long time. 'We are fighters,' he said. 'There are many of us who believe that even when losing a battle you should die fighting.'

'That has long been an honorable creed,' Perlemutter said. 'One that men have respected since the time of Sparta. But this is not your battle; it is your children's. And they cannot fight, only lose. The world is changing faster than it ever has before. This new world might not be better than the old, or even as good in some ways, but your children deserve a place in it.'

'For the children I would say yes,' Mondar admitted thoughtfully. 'But for the men — I cannot ask them to give up fighting and become sheepherders. I would as soon ask them to become sheep.'

'Perhaps,' Peter said, 'if they were willing to change just a little and adopt the new title of soldiers instead of warriors, we could stop short of asking them to become shepherds.'

Mondar eyed Peter. 'You would have us fight for you?'

Peter said, 'Jeppet will be a rich country, and many will want to have a piece of this richness any way they can. It will need a permanent border guard.'

'It would mean giving up moving and staying in this place.'

'It goes with the rest,' Peter said. 'Schools can't be moved.'

'Al-Rashid would trust us to do this?'

'If you trust him, he can do no less.'

Mondar stood up. 'This must be discussed. We will continue tomorrow. Tents have been put up for you to sleep in, as is our custom.' They went outside, picking up their rifles at the flap, and Mondar led them to the side of his tent. There a smaller version of the tent they had just left was standing. 'Yours,'

Mondar told Peter. 'One for you is on the far side,' he said to Professor Perlemutter. 'You are my guests. If you need anything, there is a bell.' He bowed to them and went off with ben Sinna.

'What now?' Peter asked.

'Get our luggage, I guess,' the Professor said. 'Then I'm going to stretch out. I never sleep well in a sleeping bag. You may do as you like.'

'Thanks,' Peter said.

They went out to the car to pick up their bags. 'What about Sara?' asked Professor Perlemutter.

Peter shrugged. 'She must be staying wherever the women's section is. I'll bring her bag along and see if I can get it to her.' He hefted the white bag along with his own.

'Careful not to violate whatever the local custom is,' the Professor said. 'Don't go sticking your head into the women's area of Mondar's tent.'

'I wouldn't think of it,' Peter assured him. 'I'll wait for them to come to me.'

'These rifles are a nuisance,' Perlemutter said, pushing his to one side so he could put the duffel bag on his shoulder, 'but I guess we'd better hang on to them.'

'How'd you ever manage on those twenty-mile hikes in the Army?' Peter asked. 'Or didn't they have them in your Army?'

'I rode on a jeep and smiled at the enlisted men,' Perlemutter said. He groaned and staggered off under his load.

Peter brought the luggage to his tent and then returned to the car. He spent the next five minutes calling Teakettle on the radio before they answered.

'Where the devil have you been?' Tony demanded.

'Talking,' Peter told him. He gave him a description of the conversation with Mondar.

'Sounds hopeful,' Tony said. 'What do you think?'

'Ask me again this time tomorrow,' Peter said. 'What's new in the palace?'

'The rest of the tanks have arrived and are being outfitted,' Tony said. 'And the small arms we ordered are here, but without ammunition. Another foul-up.'

'It's a start, anyhow,' Peter said. He

signed off and wandered back to his tent. The camp seemed empty, since the men were off somewhere discussing his proposal and the women were hidden inside their tents, presumably until the visitors had left. Peter sat at the door to his tent to catch the slight breeze that had sprung up behind the late afternoon sun and, using his handkerchief as a rag, started carefully cleaning the dust off his rifle. With a slight change in dress he could be any of the tribesmen he had seen as he came into camp that morning, sitting outside their tents polishing their long rifles.

Beyond the tents the sparse green plain stretched out in all directions, abutting suddenly against the sharp sides of the cliff-faced mountains that surrounded and protected the close. The slight breeze hardly stirred the tufted wiry plants that grew in clumps about the plain, sending their roots deep for water and baring a few small green leaves to the hot sun. There was a curious, muted, murmuring, whispering sound in the air, and far off a small dust devil danced and sparkled before the gray cliffs.

Behind Mondar's tent a woman — Peter thought it might be the one he had seen before — sat in the shade and worked at something involving cloth and thread. A small child, perhaps two years old, played silently at her side. They were half-hidden where they sat, and only when a stray gust billowed the folds of the tent could Peter see them. He thought of going to speak with her to see if he could locate Sara Quinline, but decided it would be better not to. *When in Rome*, he reminded himself, *eat spaghetti*. He started polishing the stock of his rifle, bringing out the years of linseed oil that had been hand-rubbed into the dark walnut.

Peter leaned back against the tent post and surveyed this remnant of a more primitive world. *If they accept our offer*, he thought, *all this will be changed in a few years*. He tried to picture tall white buildings in the valley, with men in Western dress — and probably briefcases under their arms — walking about. Women in short skirts, staring into store windows. Cars cluttering the street.

Perhaps a bus wheezing to a stop in front of him. Then the image burst, and he found that he could picture none of it. In some obscure way he was glad.

The sun was lower over the camp, and the shadows longer. Still the camp appeared empty, like a movie set after the day's shooting, when the actors and technicians had all gone home. He remembered a hill in northern Italy, where an Imperial Roman fortress much larger than this camp had been raised. An actress starring in the picture had invited him out to see it, and they had stayed long after the others had left, running and laughing on the Valli wall and making love on the spot where next morning an overly handsome Caesar Augustus was scheduled to address his troops.

The dust devil danced brighter and whirled its zigzag path closer to the camp. Peter could make out the individual motes of sand held up in the swirl of air, each separate yet contributing to the whole. Comprising a few thousand bits of dust — the finest desert sand, held in a random twist of air — the thing seemed to have a life and intellect of its own. It darted toward the camp and then away in a graceful pirouette, hardly disturbing the plants it passed over.

Something moved in the corner of Peter's vision. He blinked his eyes to clear the glare and refocused them. The baby, attracted by the silver motes that had come to play with it, had left the woman and was crawling in a determined line toward his airy friend. Peter glanced toward the woman, but she was engrossed in her work and didn't seem to have noticed yet that the child was gone. The proprieties of the situation gave Peter something to work out. Does one go over to a woman he is probably not supposed to see, tip his hat, and in a language she doesn't understand tell her the small child she was watching is off pursuing a bit of wind? Would his motives be understood? Should one go off, grab the child, and deposit it, no doubt squealing, in the lap of its mistress? If she knew the child to be on its jaunt, recognized the dust devil as the harmless puff of wind it was, and thought it good for a son of el

Quarat to adventure at a tender age, that would also be misunderstood, or at least unappreciated. It was probably best to keep polishing his gun and hope the woman missed the child before he was too far away.

Something else moved to the side of the babe's path as he sought his tenuous goal. Straight, slender, and with a hooded head, it stood two feet high and waved back and forth against the wind. As the child approached, it lengthened out and leaned back, its head forming a hooded arch against the sky. It paused there for a second, motionless, as the boy crawled into its long shadow.

Without conscious thought, and in what seemed like extended slow motion, Peter raised the butt of his Winchester to his shoulder. His cheek pressed against the smooth stock, and his eye sought to place the blackened blade of the front sight squarely in the notched V of the rear. Slowly, so slowly, he brought the muzzle down to where instinct and years of training placed his target. There would be no time for a second look, much less a second shot. The blade sight slid down across the tiny head as he squeezed the trigger, and the bead at the blade's tip intersected the target just as the gun went off.

The sharp crack of the rifle sounded, then echoed across the valley, bouncing from mountain to mountain as it died away. For a second all was still. Then the wail of a baby pierced the hush. *Thank God*, Peter thought. That bullet must have passed within five inches of his head! Then the woman screamed and ran out to the child, dropping in the dirt whatever she was working on.

There was a babble of loud, strident voices, and a group of men came running out of a nearby tent. Peter found that he was somehow still standing. His heart pounded rapidly and he felt incredibly weak. *Shock reaction*, he thought clinically. *If I'd missed, or been a second later . . .*

The men reached him, and someone grabbed the rifle from his hands. Someone else twisted his arms savagely behind him. His head was pulled back, and the point of a knife pricked his neck. The men crowded around him, and they all seemed to be yelling at him.

A fat face with a beard pendent thrust itself at him and screamed something sharp. 'I know how it looks,' Peter told the face, 'but I can explain everything.' Then he started laughing. He couldn't help it. His knees felt weak, and he would have collapsed if he wasn't being held up. The clinical voice inside him said *hysterical shock*, and that seemed even funnier.

The men suddenly grew silent and opened a path to him. Mondar stood there, and behind him, adjusting his belt, was a half-dressed Professor Perlemutter. The laughing spell left as quickly as it had come, and Peter just stood there. Mondar barked something to the men, who immediately let go of Peter. He wobbled for a second, then found that he could stand.

'What's this?' Mondar demanded.

'I was — ' Peter started, but he was interrupted by a shrill cry. The woman came from between the tents, running and stumbling up to Mondar. She had just gotten back, Peter realized. It seemed to him that an hour had passed, but it couldn't have been more than half a minute.

The woman was sobbing and trying to talk, but the only sound that came out was a shrill keening noise that escaped from her lips every few seconds. Clutched to her breast with one hand was the baby, and in her other hand, which she held before her, was the body of a snake. Blood still gushed from the crimson maw that had been its head, drenching her hand below and splattering her dress, but she didn't appear to notice. The snake, which she held up like a fearsome torch, was taller than she and trailed behind her as she approached. When she reached Mondar she stood before him trying to say something, but she couldn't. He stared at her and seemed to be trying to swallow. Mutely she passed him the snake, then the baby; then she fainted, collapsing in a heap on the ground.

Mondar dropped the snake and almost dropped the baby, but an old woman dashed out from the shadow of the tent and took it from him. He knelt down and picked up the woman gently in his arms. For a second he stood looking around, as though unsure what to do, but then he took her through the doors of his tent and disappeared inside.

'What happened?' Professor Perlemutter asked, peering closely at Peter.

'Well, I was — ' Peter said.

'Wait a second,' the Professor interrupted. He dashed off around the corner of Mondar's tent.

One of the men had headed off into the field, following the trail of snake blood. Now he yelled from where he was, pointing to the ground and starting to dance up and down. The rest of the men yelled back and then started pounding Peter on the back and shaking his hand. They took turns sighting through the Winchester, and all seemed very impressed. If the man was standing where the snake had been shot, as he evidently thought he was, it was about eighty yards away. Peter decided that he was a bit impressed himself.

Professor Perlemutter reappeared and went through the flap to Mondar's tent, carrying a small black bag. After a few minutes he came out again. 'Been applying a little first aid,' he said.

'What sort of first aid?' Peter asked.

'The simple sort. Just broke an ammonia capsule under the woman's nose to wake her up, then gave her a sedative to calm her down. She's fine now.'

'Very good,' Peter said.

'Come on, Mondar wants to see you,' Perlemutter said. He led Peter into the tent.

The woman was lying down on a cushion, and Mondar was sitting beside her holding her hand. She was talking softly as they came in. Mondar stood up and held out a hand to Peter. 'Mina has told me,' he said. 'There are no words.'

Peter took the hand and released it. 'The boy is something to you?'

'My son. Mina is my wife.'

'Oh,' Peter said, for want of anything better. 'Yes. Well, I was just lucky. I'm glad I was there.' He turned to the Professor. 'I guess it's about time we went to bed.'

'My son was lucky,' Mondar called after them as they left the tent. 'There are no words.'

Peter went back to his tent and stretched out on the bedding. He found that he couldn't sleep, so he arranged the flashlight at the top of his bed and pulled an old paperback mystery out of his bag. The book was one that he'd found on the bookshelf of the palace guest room he had slept in. It was called *Mister Pepper Finds the Body*, and had a cover picture that showed Mister Pepper leaning over what must be the body, with a young lady either dressing or undressing in the background. It was done in faded primary colors and had a notice to the effect that the 'Murder Diagram' was on the back. Peter turned the book over, and sure enough there was the Murder Diagram: an architect's drawing of a house with a large X-marked body found here. The book was close to twenty-five years old, and the yellowed pages fell out as Peter turned them. He settled down to read.

'The master would like something?' a silvery voice asked.

Peter looked up. Standing within the moonlight in his room was a female figure in a diaphanous — well, whatever it was, it was very diaphanous, and she was very female.

'Who?' he said. 'What — '

She took a step closer, the folds of her diaphanous whatever rustling delightfully. 'I was sent to find out if the master requires anything. Besides, I'm supposed to sleep here.'

'Supposed to — ' Peter didn't seem to be able to finish any sentences this evening.

The woman giggled.

'Sara!' Peter said.

'Of course, silly. Who else did you think they'd send in to sleep with you?'

'To tell you the truth . . . ' Peter said. 'Look — what's this all about?'

'My fault,' Sara said, coming over and sitting on the edge of the bed. Peter could smell her perfume. 'I called you 'master' when we got here, and they thought I meant it. They think I'm your concubine or something.' She giggled again.

'Well, why didn't you say something?'

'I didn't want to queer the act, if you'll excuse the expression. Besides . . . ' She paused. 'Well, anyway, here I am.'

'Oh,' Peter said. 'Well, I suppose I can move to the foot of the bed and give you — '

'Don't,' Sara interrupted, 'be silly. We're both civilized adults. I'll just take this side of the bed, or whatever you call this.'

'Fair enough,' Peter said, moving over to give her room. 'Did you hear anything about your brother?'

'He's not here,' Sara said. 'I'm sure of that. They don't take captives.'

'We'll find him,' Peter promised, deciding not to remind her what they did with the captives they didn't take.

'I hope so,' Sara said, snuggling down on her side of the bed. 'He's got to be somewhere.'

'True,' Peter said. He decided that for his own peace of mind he'd better try to ignore her, so he tucked the pillow under his head and went back to the book.

'Is that what you do all night?' Sara asked. 'I mean, read books?'

'I'm trying to ignore you,' Peter said firmly.

'Well,' Sara pouted, 'if that's the way you feel about it . . . ' She turned over on her stomach and, with her chin propped up on her hands, stared off at something ahead of her.

'Now look,' Peter said, 'I'm trying to ignore you because I find you very desirable and don't want to do anything I'll regret.' There, he thought, that should shut her up.

'Would you really regret it so much?' she asked softly.

Peter put his book down.

★ ★ ★

The next morning Peter came drowsily awake to find Sara, alert and happy, lying on her side and staring at him. 'Hello,' she said, seeing his eyes open.

'Hello. How are you?'

'Wonderful.' She bent over and kissed him.

'Yes,' he agreed, 'you are.' He managed to roll over and sit up.

'Is that the gun?' she asked, looking at the Winchester leaning against the wall of the tent.

'What gun?'

'With which you slew the dragon, my gentle Sir Galahad.'

'Oh,' he said. 'Yes. Where were you during all the excitement?'

'Taking a bath,' she told him. 'Or, at any rate, a sponge bath. I wanted to be clean and fresh for you.'

'How far in advance — ' Peter began, staring at her.

'A woman always knows,' she told him. 'She has to decide in advance if she wants a man, since she has to assume that he wants her and would be insulted if he didn't. Whatever a man may think, a woman is seldom seduced.'

'You,' Peter said, grabbing Sara and pulling her to him, 'are — '

'Ahem!' Professor Perlemutter was standing in the doorway to the tent.

'Good morning, Professor,' Peter said. 'You might make a little noise when you enter a strange tent.'

'I did,' Perlemutter said, 'several times.

I hadn't thought this was a strange tent, but I apologize.' He watched with frank interest and no shame while Sara rolled frantically over and pulled up the sheet.

Peter started laughing. Sara glared at him, the sheet up to her nose. 'What are you laughing at?' she demanded.

'I'm sorry,' he gasped. 'I'm not laughing at you, but the situation. The Professor is usually the soul of discretion. He walked in by accident. Would have walked out again. We never would have known. But he wanted to pay you back. To get even for your calling him 'Ziggie,'' Peter said. 'One unfair advantage deserves another.'

'Oh,' Sara said weakly. She lowered the sheet to her chin. 'Are we even?' she asked the Professor.

Perlemutter bowed slightly. 'I will even admit to having the better of it. The memory of pleasure to the eye will quite overbalance the memory of harshness to the ear.'

'Oh,' Sara said, lowering the sheet a bit more. 'That's quite nice.'

'Enough compliments,' Peter said, 'or you'll have the sheet off her again.'

'That's not so,' Sara said indignantly. 'If you'll turn around for a second, Ziggie, I'll go get dressed.'

'Of course,' the Professor said, and instantly turned his back and started to study the tent pole with interest. Sara's long legs flashed as she rose from behind the sheet and disappeared behind an ornate wall of tenting.

The Professor beamed at Peter. 'I think we've done it.'

'Done it?'

'Convinced Mondar,' Perlemutter explained. 'I saw him this morning, and he wants to speak with us after we eat'

'That's wonderful,' Sara called from behind the screen. 'Would someone pass me my suitcase?'

The Professor lugged the white bag over to the screen and handed it through.

'How did he look?' Peter asked, getting up and hunting through his duffel bag for fresh clothes. 'Pleased?'

'About half-pleased, half-apprehensive about having made the right decision, and half-satisfied that the decision was made, if you know what I mean.'

'I'm not sure I do,' Peter said, fishing out a pair of socks. 'There seem to be too many halfs in there to suit me.'

* * *

A large breakfast tray was brought in by a youth who, in Sara's translation, wished them all long life and then departed. The tray held a large teapot and a larger plate holding flaky rolls that had been doused with honey.

After breakfast Professor Perlemutter got up from his cross-legged seat on the cushion and stretched. 'We'd best find Mondar.'

Peter agreed. 'What are you going to do?' he asked Sara.

'I'll go talk to Mina,' she said. 'We've got quite friendly. Set up a sort of information exchange. I'm learning a lot about native customs from her.'

'I'm sure she's learning a lot about native customs from you,' Peter said. 'See you later.'

Finding Mondar proved to be easy. There was a man waiting outside the tent to take them to him. He was in a tent across the way, conducting a sort of arms inspection. There, on a carpet in front of him, a recoilless rifle had been separated neatly into its few component parts.

'As-salaamu alaykum,' he said as they entered. 'I hope you slept well.'

'Wa-alaikum-salaam,' Peter finished the ritual greeting. 'Very well, thank you.'

'I thought you didn't speak Arabic,' Mondar said, a glint of suspicion in his eye.

'You've just heard all the Arabic I speak,' Peter told him.

'Of course,' Mondar said. 'It's hard to stay in this part of the world and not learn at least that much. It's just my idea of the provincialism of English speakers that they refuse to learn any language other than their own.'

'It's basically true,' Peter admitted. 'One who knows the language of Shakespeare and Damon Runyon doesn't seem to feel that learning any other is worthwhile. Although I admit that few of us speak our language with anything of the grace of either of those gentlemen.'

'Damon Runyon?' Mondar asked.

'A recent stylist,' Peter told him. He promised, at Mondar's request, to send a sample of Runyon's work. 'The provincialism is easily explained,' he said. 'English is the language of an island people and a people who had almost a whole continent to travel in without having to change languages. Those of us who work much in other lands usually pick up a few languages, although we never become as fluent in them as we might. There are always people around who speak English. In Europe or here, where you constantly rub shoulders with those using other tongues, it's to be expected that you'd be multilingual. I speak four languages fairly well. The Professor speaks, I believe, seven, but he was blessed with a childhood in Europe.'

'Seven?' Mondar asked Perlemutter, sounding impressed.

'Let's see.' Perlemutter mumbled to himself for a second. 'Eight, and several dialects.'

'Splendid,' Mondar said. 'I myself have five.' He turned and waved a hand toward the gun. 'What do you think of her?' he asked.

'A fine weapon,' Peter said. 'I believe I've seen a sample of its effect.'

'Ah, yes,' Mondar said. 'The station. Well, if we're to work together it will be differently employed in the future.'

That, Peter decided, was the most casual formal agreement he had ever heard announced. 'That would be fine,' he said carefully.

'These,' Mondar said, indicating a few empty cartridge cases piled to one side. 'Can they be reloaded?'

'Yes,' Peter said, 'but it takes special equipment.'

'We are quite adept at reloading bullets,' Mondar said.

'I'll bet,' Peter answered, picturing el Quarat picking up their spent brass as they attacked a fort. 'I'll see that you get the equipment as soon as possible. And, probably, more of these weapons, although of a different caliber.'

'That would be good,' Mondar said. 'Now, I assume there is something specific you want us to do in regard to the

Desert Legion. Something to establish our commitment. My men would be willing to attempt an all-out attack on their camp, but that does not seem altogether advisable.'

'There is something,' Peter admitted, ceasing to wonder at Mondar's acute perception, 'but not quite that drastic.' He outlined the plan for handling the legion and described el Quarat's place in it.

Mondar asked a few questions, then thought deeply for a minute. 'Agreed,' he said, holding out his hand. Peter shook it, then Professor Perlemutter shook it, and the formalities were ended.

'How long can you stay?' Mondar asked.

'We should leave as soon as possible,' Peter told him, 'but we'll come back.'

'I'll hold you to that. You must have lunch with us today, and then you can leave.'

Lunch was held in the clearing among the tents. Several hundred people distributed themselves on cushions that had been set out in a large circle. Peter noticed that for the first time there were many women among them.

Mondar sat at one point on the circle, thus showing the democracy of the gathering since a circle has no head. On his left sat Mina, and on his right, Sara. He must have soon regretted the arrangement, because the two women spent the whole meal chattering and gesturing back and forth while he sat impassively between them. To Sara's right sat Peter, then Professor Perlemutter. To Mina's left sat ben Sinna.

After the meal, which was simple, although much better than the chicken à la king that is standard at American luncheons, Mondar stood up. He spoke for a long time, softly and easily, and the men listened.

'What's he saying?' Peter whispered to Sara.

'He's stating in formal terms the agreement the tribe has come to with you. It's the equivalent of the signing of the treaty. He'll ask them if they agree to this, and they'll all say yes. It's a formality, since it was decided last night. Congratulations.'

'Thanks,' Peter said.

Mondar finished speaking, and there was a hushed silence over the gathering. Then all at once, the assemblage shouted something that sounded like 'arribat' but probably wasn't. Then another short silence, and Mondar started speaking again.

'What now?' Peter whispered.

'He's talking about you,' Sara answered, but she wouldn't say any more.

Mondar took the two steps over to where Peter sat. 'Stand up,' he said. Peter, feeling like a guest speaker who has suddenly discovered that he's at the wrong banquet, stood up. Mondar said something more and put his hand on Peter's shoulder. A great shout went up. He took a small, thin knife from his belt and held it before him, glittering in the sunlight. Another shout. Mondar suddenly grabbed Peter's right arm and pricked the wrist with his knife.

'What — ' Peter started, as a large drop of blood formed over the cut.

Mondar pricked his own wrist and took Peter's arm. They stood there a minute like Roman centurions shaking hands, blood mixing with blood. A drop fell and was soaked up by the dry ground. Peter thought he understood.

'Try not to look so startled,' Mondar said, smiling. 'We are now blood brothers.'

Peter also smiled. 'You could have warned me, my brother.'

They released hands, and Mondar kissed him quickly on both cheeks. The men cheered. 'You saved my child's life,' Mondar said, 'and you are now its uncle and godfather.'

The child was brought out for Peter to admire, which he dutifully did, and then was taken away. Peter, in a sudden gesture, unslung his rifle and handed it to Mondar. 'A gift,' he said, 'between brothers.'

Mondar was delighted. He took off his own rifle and presented it to Peter. 'My son will have this when he comes of age,' he promised, slinging the rifle over his shoulder. 'In his name, I thank you.'

Peter and Mondar sat down again. This seemed to end the lunch, as people started drifting away. 'Well,' Peter said, 'I suppose we'd better get packed and leave.'

'I've already packed us,' Sara told him. 'We're all set.'

'You're a wonder. I think I'll adopt you.'

Sara giggled. 'I'll make out the papers.'

'First I have to find a way to get you to stop giggling.'

'That will come with maturity,' Professor Perlemutter offered. 'I imagine she'll giggle very seldom when she's sixty.'

'Nonsense,' Sara insisted. 'It's a hereditary trait.'

They stood up. Mondar rose with them. 'All has been said,' he stated, shaking hands with each of them again. 'You are welcome here at any time. Please come back.'

'We will,' Peter promised.

'My wife has become very fond of you,' Mondar told Sara. 'You also return.'

'I shall,' Sara assured him.

Everyone in the camp lined up to watch the car as they drove away. They received a cavalry escort as far as the entrance to the trail, and there the men left them, hands upraised in farewell. Sara waved until they were out of sight. 'Nice people,' she said.

'Yes,' Peter agreed.

'Here,' Sara said, 'let me wash the blood off your wrist. I didn't think I should do it until we'd left the camp.'

'You're probably right,' Peter agreed, holding out his arm. She wet a piece of sterile cotton with water from a water bag and wiped off Peter's arm. 'It's just a pinprick,' she told him. 'You won't even need a bandage.'

'That's good.'

The Professor asked thoughtfully, 'How much of their ease of agreement do you think was due to the fortuitous circumstance of your affair with the viper?'

'I don't imagine it hurt,' Peter said, 'but I think they wouldn't have been overly swayed by it. They would have decided the same way anyhow. The only thing I got out of that was a hole in my wrist.'

'I think I agree,' Perlemutter said.

'Don't make fun of that blood-brother ceremony,' Sara said. 'They really mean that. If you were ever in serious trouble, Mondar would sell anything but his wife and risk his life to help you.'

'I know that,' Peter said. 'I wasn't making fun of it; I'm very impressed.'

They rounded a turn in the road and found a great log blocking their way. 'Where'd that come from?' Professor Perlemutter asked.

'It ain't natural,' Peter told him. He braked the car and reached for his pistol. Before he could get it out, a small grinning face appeared in the open window. Peter's fist shot out, hitting the face square on the jaw, and it snapped back and toppled over.

Someone jumped up on the other side of the car, but Professor Perlemutter, with surprising agility, released the door handle and slammed the door outward with his feet, knocking his assailant off the running board and leaving him sprawled senseless on the road.

'What next?' Peter asked, pistol in his hand.

'Counter-attack,' Perlemutter suggested, pulling his carbine around and snapping a round into the chamber. 'We're nesting quail in this car.'

'That's 'sitting ducks.' Stick to the idiom. However, you have a good point. Let's go.'

'What do I do?' asked Sara, who seemed more excited than frightened.

'Keep down,' Peter said. He and the Professor left the car and stalked cautiously around to the front, eying the log.

Several tennis-ball-like objects sailed through the air toward them, hissing as they came. They dropped, and Peter let off a couple of quick shots when he thought he saw a motion behind the log. The balls landed, bounced, rolled, and kept hissing.

'Gas,' Peter said. 'Let's get out of here!'

Before they could get up, the balls gave off a popping sound, and a cloud of thin green smoke enveloped them. It seemed to Peter, with his last waking thought, that he was falling very slowly through the stars toward the center of the galaxy.

13

Commander-General Brontke had his men lined up before him for their morning pep talk. He strode back and forth on the small platform, eying with some secret emotion the rows of men standing at attention before him. 'You men,' he announced to the spotless uniforms, 'are the finest fighting force since Rommel's North Africa Command.' He leaned forward. 'I know. I was there.' He gripped the sides of the lectern, his knuckles showing white. 'And we would have won, too, if it wasn't for that stupid swine with the mustache and all his pathetic aides. We would have won!' he screamed. 'And now we will win. We will win!'

He stopped and got control of himself. 'I have created you from the scum of the earth, and you are my instrument. In four days we attack Akr. Within forty-eight hours all of Jeppet will be ours. That is my plan, and it cannot fail.' His voice grew loud and shrill, and he trembled visibly. 'And that is only the beginning!'

Some of the men, carried away by the power of his voice, saw a shaking giant up there on the stand. Then he shrunk to normal size and the shaking ceased. 'There will be a staff meeting in the command tent,' he said in a soft voice, and turned around to leave the stand.

'Dismissed,' a sergeant shouted, and the even ranks dissolved into little groups of men hurrying to their jobs.

Lieutenant Khazar hurried around to the different orderly rooms to collect the daily morning reports, glad of a job that would keep him away from the general for even a short while. The routine should save him from the general's attentions when he got back. Take the seven filled-out forms back to his desk and look busy and intent while he correlated the useless information: so many men on duty, so many men sick, no men AWOL or deserting (where would they go?), so many men reprimanded for this or that minor infraction of General Brontke's long list of regulations. Then he'd type up the master morning report on his ancient typewriter and put it on Brontke's desk. The general would read it over carefully, make a pointedly nasty remark about Khazar's typing, and then hand it back to him to be safely filed in a folder marked 'Current Status.' He would take the last morning report from the folder and file it in the archives file under 'Morning Reports, Recent.' When that got too full, he would take the oldest month's reports out of it and file them in one of the cardboard file cartons by their date. No one would ever look at any of these reports, but the general seemed to have the traditional German feeling that you could do anything you wanted to as long as the paperwork was correct.

When Lieutenant Khazar returned to the command tent, clutching the flimsy forms, which were badly printed in illegible handwriting by the illiterate first sergeants (and the one who was literate but knew better than to admit it), one of General Brontke's famous scenes was in progress. The object of the scene this time, as usual, was his favorite whipping boy, Colonel Bahar. The officers were grouped around the general's sandbox and stood uncomfortably at ease while Brontke, at the head of the box, laced into Bahar at the foot. Khazar, observing bitterly that he'd have to pass in front of Colonel Bahar to get to his desk, stood nervously in the doorway.

'You have it wrong, Colonel, as usual,' Brontke said caustically, pointing to the war toys in the box. 'During that salvo my tank destroyed yours and came through undamaged.'

'B-but General — ' Bahar said.

'Are you arguing with me?' Brontke demanded, squinting at Bahar. 'Do you question my impartiality as umpire of these games?'

'N-no, sir.'

Khazar had heard him question not only that but also the general's sanity, but only in private after a few drinks.

'Then what is it?'

Careful, Lieutenant Khazar thought, *or we'll all be in trouble.*

'I just thought you could explain your opinion to us,' Bahar said. 'Since both tanks fired at once, it would seem that both tanks should be considered destroyed.

221

There's obviously something wrong with my reasoning, and if you'd explain it, I'd know in the future.'

'Your reasoning!' Brontke snorted. 'Your — ha! It's perfectly clear if you'd just look.' He pointed a quavering finger. 'Look at the tanks. You see?'

Colonel Bahar bent over for a closer look at the two models. 'W . . . what?' he asked.

'My tank,' Brontke said triumphantly, 'is bigger than your tank!' There was a silence in the room while everyone digested this. 'See? See?' Brontke asked, scuttling around the table and grabbing the two tanks. He thrust them under Colonel Bahar's nose.

Khazar could see from where he stood that the two models, plastic children's toys that had been assembled lovingly from kits by the general and painstakingly painted in the colors and insignia of the World War Two German and British armies, had indeed been designed on slightly different scales. The general's model was a bit larger than Colonel Bahar's. An old children's doggerel song ran unbidden through Khazar's mind as he watched the tableau. 'My dog's bigger than your dog,' it went. 'My dog's bigger than yours.' He ignored it.

'Why, of c-course,' Bahar said, staring at the two tanks beneath his nose. 'Your tank is quite a bit bigger than mine. It was hard to see in the perspective of the sand, er, Simulated Battle Area.'

'Well,' General Brontke said, slightly mollified, 'see that you notice in the future.' Carefully replacing the tanks, he strode back to his position on the board and adjusted his cap to a jaunty angle. 'Men,' he said, picking up a dummy microphone and holding it to his lips, 'resume the engagement!'

A tape recorder was turned on behind the general, and the rumble of tanks filled the room. The aides pushed the models to their new positions in the continuing battle. Brontke and Colonel Bahar gave orders into their microphones, and the models were wheeled and shifted about. The deafening crump of heavy tank guns and the chatter of machine guns issued from the tape recorder as the mock battle proceeded. Lieutenant Khazar hurried to his desk and started shuffling the meaning-less reports around. He took some aspirins from a large bottle in his top drawer and chewed on them while making cryptic marks on the onionskin papers.

A runner dashed into the tent, danced around the busy officers, and stationed himself at attention by the general's side, waiting to be noticed. Commander-General Pertival Hals Von-und-Zu Brontke made a gesture, and the war machine was shut off in mid-roar. 'Well, what is it?' he yelped.

'Begging the general's pardon,' the runner said, giving a stiff salute, 'but the weekly plane is landing.'

General Brontke returned the salute. 'Very good.'

The runner took two steps backward, saluted again, wheeled, and ran into a post. He staggered, shook his head, and lurched out of the tent.

'Very good boy,' the general said, star-ing after him. 'Perhaps a trifle overzealous.'

Just in a hurry to get away from you, Lieutenant Khazar thought very silently.

'Everyone dismissed — we will con-tinue later,' Brontke said. The officers quickly cleared the tent, leaving Lieutenant Khazar alone with General Von-and-Zu. 'You're here,' the general said with some surprise. 'When did you come in? No matter, cover the simulator and go escort General Harry here.'

Lieutenant Khazar covered the sandbox with a large canvas, leaving it looking like a lumpy pool table, and hurried through the door. The twin-engine cargo plane, painted a dull olive with no markings, was taxiing along the strip of desert that served as a runway. It came about once a week, on an irregular schedule, bringing supplies, two-week-old mail from the Swiss post box that was their address, an occasional recruit, and the mysterious general — code named Harry — who was their contact with the government that secretly supported them. No man except General Brontke even knew what that government was.

The plane stopped as Khazar approached it. The hatch opened and an aluminum ladder snaked out to the ground. General Harry, son of the famous Mata Harry, Khazar guessed, climbed stiffly to the ground.

General Harry, an incredibly gross man in civilian clothes — an expensively tailored Western-style suit that clung damply to him, exposing vast amounts of white-shirt-clad belly — was mopping his face with a square yard of pink handkerchief when Lieutenant Khazar reached him.

'Good morning, Lieutenant,' Harry said, puffing cheerfully. 'I seem to be a bit out of breath from descending that ladder. I must be getting a trifle overweight. Just a trifle, I fancy. What do you say?'

'This way, sir,' Lieutenant Khazar said, refusing to be baited.

'Ah, Lieutenant, admirably silent and single-purposed. I admire you, I really do,' Harry said, trotting alongside Lieutenant Khazar and puffing as he spoke.

Brontke was sitting at his desk with the chair pushed back. 'Ah, General,' he said, standing as they came in. 'Good to see you; sit down, sit down.' He pulled out a chair, which Harry lowered himself gingerly into, then returned to his own seat. 'How are things on the home front?'

Home front? Khazar wondered. The general sounded a bit strange.

'Everyone is proceeding well,' code-name Harry said smoothly.

'Fine, fine,' Brontke said. 'Here, have a cigar and a bit of schnapps with me.' He extracted a brown earthenware bottle and two glasses from a drawer along with a box of cigars.

'My religion forbids it,' Harry said, leaning back, 'but indulge yourself by all means.'

'Your religion — ' Brontke said, sounding for a moment like a bewildered old man. But then he caught himself. 'Of course, what was I thinking of? For a moment I thought . . . ' He shook his head. 'Lieutenant, bring the general some coffee. Or would you prefer tea?'

'Coffee will do fine, thank you,' General Harry said. Khazar raced over to the mess tent and came back loaded with coffee, canned milk and sugar.

'Very good, Lieutenant, thank you,' Harry said, smiling as Khazar placed the tray on the desk in front of him. 'Now, where were we?' He poured himself a cup of coffee and added sugar to the cup until the whole was a thick syrup, then stirred the sludge thoughtfully. 'You're ready to go, you say, General?'

'Four days,' Brontke said, 'and we strike!' He slammed his palm down on the table.

'Good, good,' Harry said, wincing slightly. 'Fine. Excellent.'

'My special tanks,' Brontke said, leaning forward, his eyes seeming even closer to his nose. 'Where are they?'

'They were landed at a secret place four days ago and have been coming here in convoy with the last of the gasoline since then. We overflew them as we came in, and our timing was good. They're about four or five miles out now, and I should be able to take the drivers back with me. They're my boys. You do have drivers of your own, I trust?' he asked, leaning forward in turn so that his nose was an inch from Brontke's.

Brontke leaned back quickly. *Harry has bad breath*, Khazar decided. *I've seen the ads*.

'Yes,' Brontke said. 'My men are all well trained. Here, look.' He crossed over to the sandbox and twitched the canvas off. 'Here we are, and here they are,' he said, pointing to each group of tanks in turn. 'That's my tank in the lead.' He picked up the toy and held it out for General Harry to inspect. 'That's me in the cupola — see the insignia?'

'Yes, of course,' Harry said, sounding a little puzzled. He glanced over at Lieutenant Khazar, who averted his eyes.

'It's all planned out, every detail,' Brontke said, speaking quickly and precisely. 'That's what's important, the details. Everything must be known and allowed for in advance. There must be no mistakes. I will allow no mistakes.'

'Very good,' Harry said. 'Excellent. I will report so to my superiors.' To Khazar, he sounded doubtful.

'Good, good,' Brontke said, sounding pleased. 'Tell them there will be no mistakes.'

'They will be pleased,' Harry said vaguely.

'Listen,' Brontke said. 'They're here.'

'I don't hear anything,' Harry said.

'They're here,' Brontke insisted. 'My tanks are here!' He raced outside.

General Harry and Lieutenant Khazar joined him quickly. From outside the tent they could just make out the sound of heavy engines in the distance. General Brontke, looking every inch the Wehrmacht commander, strode proudly off toward the sound. Lieutenant Khazar, with Harry puffing at his side, followed behind. As they went, the men in camp, attracted by the increasing sound, fell in behind.

They left the camp and marched out into the desert, the men in an unsteady battle line behind them. Suddenly, from over the crest of a hillock in front of them, a giant tank appeared. The juggernaut rose up for an incredible distance, its treads clawing the air, and then fell forward and ground toward them. A second tank followed, looking like a ghostly mirage in the thick dust cloud of the first, and then came a third and a fourth. Behind them, like a string of Lilliputians following four Gullivers, were the ten-ton transports in a tight convoy.

Lieutenant Khazar took an involuntary step backward. 'What in the — ' He swallowed. 'What are those?'

'Tanks, my boy,' General Harry said. 'Tiger tanks, Hitler's secret weapon.

Ninety tons of armor-plated monster. A little slow and unwieldy, but once they get into battle, it's over. They can't be transported by rail and can't go over most bridges, so they weren't much use in Europe where Hitler tried them, but the desert's their meat.' Harry chuckled and then whispered in Lieutenant Khazar's ear, as if imparting a special secret, 'That's if they don't break down!'

General Brontke stood there on the sand, his feet apart, hands at his sides, breathing deeply and watching the Tiger tanks approach. 'They're here,' he said softly. 'They're here,' he crooned. Then he clenched his fist and shouted at the heavens, 'They're here! We're invincible. Nothing can stop us now.'

'They're here,' Harry said, mopping beads of sweat from his forehead, chin and neck. 'That's right, General.'

Brontke turned slowly around. 'Today Jeppet,' he said, a glazed look in his eyes. 'Tomorrow . . . '

'That's right, General,' Harry said, patting him on the back. 'That's right, General Brontke.'

14

'Anything new?'

Eric Jurgens swiveled his chair to face the questioner. '*Nyet, nada, de rien, nichts, neues,* no. No word at all. They seem to have vanished.'

Tony Ryan eased himself into a chair across the desk. 'What about the car?'

'Not a trace.' He pulled out a pack of English cigarettes and offered one to Tony.

Tony tamped the cigarette on the edge of the desk and then lit it. 'What do you think of Mondar?'

'I believe him. It fits in with what Peter told us the last time we contacted him.' Eric shrugged. 'I think we'll have to look somewhere else for an answer.'

'We will,' Tony said firmly. 'We'll by-god look everywhere in this damn desert.' He unhappily examined the blue smoke twirling up from his cigarette. 'Disappearing seems to be the thing to do around here.'

'More so than you know,' Eric told

him. 'When we talked to Mondar, he said that agents of the Desert Legion were up asking about the officer who delivered their last load of supplies. They seemed convinced el Quarat had done away with him.'

'Another mystery,' Tony said. 'Well, at least it seems to hit both sides. I'd begun to wonder if maybe the legion hadn't engineered this one.'

'They may have at that,' Eric reminded him.

'True,' Tony admitted, 'but somehow I doubt it. It seems a bit too subtle for them.'

'I agree,' Eric said.

'Still, we shouldn't forget the possibility.'

'We won't.'

There was a knock on the partly open office door, and Smyth-Black, the British brigadier, stuck his head around the corner. 'You chaps busy?' he asked.

'Never too busy to greet a colleague,' Eric said. 'Tony, break out the Coca-Cola.'

Smyth-Black shuddered. 'No, thank

you,' he said. 'Never touch the stuff.'

Tony hauled a familiar green bottle out of the bottom drawer of the filing cabinet, along with three glasses, and poured three fingers of amber fluid into each glass. 'Cheers,' he said, passing one to the brigadier.

Smyth-Black sniffed suspiciously at the glass. 'Scotch?' he queried.

'I see you have an infallible nose,' Tony said. 'We keep it in this disguise so as not to inadvertently offend our hosts, who follow the Islam persuasion.'

'Scotch,' Brigadier Smyth-Black sighed. 'And you don't even follow the barbaric American custom of icing it.' He relaxed into a hardback chair and allowed a pleased smile to waver along the thin edge of lip that showed under his mustache.

'Are you ready to relinquish the controls of government?' Eric asked.

'Official ceremony's all set for Wednesday, four days from now,' Smyth-Black said. 'Then we sail away into the night, divested of one more spot of Empire over which the sun had such trouble setting.'

'Leaving Jeppet a free country,' Tony

said, 'for as long as it lasts.'

'Oh,' Smyth-Black said, 'yes. You'll be glad to hear that those Hornets you looked so covetously at will be left accidentally behind when we leave.'

'Accidentally?' asked Eric.

'Well,' the brigadier said, looking embarrassed, 'the red tape involved in getting official permission is liable to extend until our next election, so I'm going to manage to misinterpret one of my orders. By the time it's straightened out you should be able to keep them.'

'With luck,' Tony said, 'we won't need them anymore. Thank you. May the god of battle smile on you.' He lifted his glass in toast.

Smyth-Black looked embarrassed. 'Accidents will happen, you know, in the best regulated armies.'

'True,' Tony admitted. 'Dreadful. How large an accident do you think this will be?'

'About nine Hornets,' Smyth-Black estimated into his glass. 'With four Malkara missiles each.'

'Propitious accident,' Eric said. 'Are the

things easy to operate?'

'Deucedly complicated,' Brigadier Smyth-Black said. 'Incidentally, not that there's any connection, but nine of our young officers have requested permission to take leave here for a short time after we pull out. They all seem to have some sort of unfinished business here. Do you think it could be arranged? All in mufti, of course. Don't want to give anyone cause for complaint.'

'Of course,' Eric said suspiciously. 'Nine?'

'Yes. By some odd chance they're all crew chiefs on the Hornets.'

'Peculiar,' Tony admitted. 'We'll take care of them.'

'Good,' Smyth-Black said, draining his glass and getting up. 'I'd send them along. Do keep them out of trouble, will you?' He ambled out the door without waiting for an answer.

'That's a splendid example of something or other,' Tony said.

Eric nodded. 'It is. Things are looking up.'

'They are?' Tony asked. 'What sort of

things?' He looked around.

'Well,' Eric said, waving his hand, 'telescopes, for example.'

John Wander ran in through the opened door. 'They're back,' he yelped, collapsing into the empty chair.

'Who?' Tony demanded.

'Peter,' John gasped, pointing his finger down the empty hall, 'and the Professor and the woman. They just drove up downstairs.'

'Where've they been?' Tony asked at the same time that Eric yelled, 'What happened to them?'

'It's quite a story,' John said.

15

He was fully awake, with no knowledge of how long he'd been that way. It seemed very important to figure that out, but memories of the recent past kept flooding in and disrupting his thinking. He remembered hearing colors and watching music. He had the feeling that there was something wrong with that, but he couldn't decide what. Time seemed to be stretched out in front of him like a series of soap bubbles fastened to a glittering string. Each time bubble popped softly as he entered it, and enveloped him. All things seemed equally apart inside, until the soft blub when he left one bubble and waited outside of time for the next to reach him.

Several eternities passed.

I should move my right hand, he decided. He sent commands. They marched down the nerve train from his brain to the spinal cord, where they got in a long argument with some information coming up from his left foot, and then proceeded along the shoulder to the arm. From arm to elbow to hand they flew, and he was pleased to feel the fingers wiggle. He could see them wiggle, too, he found, and discovered that his arm was stretched out in front of him. That's silly, he thought, and the arm fell to his side.

His left foot itched. It was a problem in logistics. He thought about it for some time. His left foot itched. He sent an extra load of blood to the spot to relieve the itching and resumed the exploration of each process of his body. His lungs. He watched them expand and contract, holding his breath and expelling it in little puffs.

'Here, drink!'

He looked up. A long brown hand was extended to him, holding a small glass with some colorless liquid. He examined the hand.

'Here, drink?' The hand seemed quite insistent. His left foot itched. He took the small amount of liquid in his mouth while trying to decide what to do about the foot. The hand went away.

Scratch, he thought. It was a marvelous invention. He sat up and ran his finger over the bottom of his foot. It tickled.

He lay back and continued to explore the possibilities of his vast body, which seemed to take up most of the universe. There was something about the universe, but he couldn't remember. After a while the exploration reached his brain, and he lay watching the neurons passing messages back and forth. *It's changed*, he thought. *It's making new paths.* He tried to decide what was different. Something about color and sound and hearing. He played with the senses.

Awareness of his surroundings filtered through a veil of contrasting information. Recent memory was as important as present fact, but recent memory was vague and unrelated. There was some bit of information from some separate and untouchable part of his mind that was fighting for attention. It beat like waves on his thoughts: breaking on his conscious mind, making sense and commanding vital importance for a second, then disappearing in a mist of unremembered droplets until the next breaker. He reached for the thought, and finally he held it. *I've been drugged*, it yelled.

'Oh.' He relaxed. 'So that's it.' He was glad to find it out. Some bit of information that went with it, something to do about it, was lost in his brain.

He rolled off the bed and, giggling, fell to the floor. His hands reached for the buckle on his belt. The buckle broke apart and little round colored things rolled onto the floor.

Which ones? the other part of him wondered.

'The green ones are a pretty shape,' he offered, 'but the red ones are too loud.'

Which ones?

He considered. 'The light gray ones and the white ones with the X, of course.'

He sat up on the floor and picked up all the others, putting them carefully back into the buckle holder. Several times they spilled out and he had to start all over, but finally he made it. He screwed the top back on and stared at the floor. 'Those.'

There were nine left: four of the gray

ones and five of the scored white ones. He considered them carefully.

Take them?

He put one of the gray ones in his mouth and chewed. It tasted gray. He swallowed and carefully selected another.

After the fourth pill they didn't taste gray anymore, only bitter, and he gulped the rest of them down quickly.

He sat there staring at the floor and not moving for some time. At first the pattern seemed to swallow him, but then he withdrew into himself and the pattern receded. His body changed from a collection of parts to an organic whole and then was just a body, framework for his brain. He felt normal and one, and became aware of his identity.

I've been drugged, he thought again, and it made sense. He didn't want to do anything, didn't want to move, but his mind was working. *I've been under some powerful hallucinogen. I've certainly been having hallucinations.* He remembered his recent experiences as best as he could and tried to decide which were real and which were fantasy. He couldn't. He remembered the hand and the stuff he drank, then remembered that he didn't drink it. *That's it*, he decided. *Their mistake.* He wondered who 'they' were. The pills his subconscious — or, perhaps, superconscious — had prodded him into taking, tranquilizers, had done the rest of the job, bringing him down from the heights of happy introspection. They'd left him feeling like a vegetable, with no desire even to move, but at least they'd normalized his thinking. He waited to see what would happen next.

After a while two men came in carrying a bed. It had handles at both ends like a sedan chair, a soft mattress, feet to keep it off the ground, and a folded-back canopy overhead. They lifted him gently from his sitting position on the floor and put him on the bed.

'Drink this,' a voice he recognized said, and one of the men held out a glass to him. He took it and filled his mouth. Then they lifted the bed and started down a long corridor, gently swaying the bed as they walked in step. Peter had the feeling he'd made the trip before, but he couldn't remember. He rolled over on the bed and released the liquid from his mouth, hoping it wouldn't stain the pillow. They didn't notice.

The bed was brought into a large room, where the men put it down and left. Peter, still prone on his stomach and staring into the pillow, heard noises. *I should look around*, he thought. He didn't move. *I must turn over*, he thought. He still didn't move. *This is silly*, he decided. *Nobody can be this tranquil*. He willed himself to roll over, and his body responded as though it were fighting its way through syrup.

Once over, he lay still on his back. His eyes darted eagerly around, although his body didn't move. The room stretched away in all directions: even the ceiling was far above him. Water ran through a channel cut into the floor and ended in a pool from which a fountain sprayed the air. Peter tried to remember when he'd been here before. It was very hazy, and mixed with the memory of some tremendously important discovery that he couldn't quite remember.

There were women sitting around the pool. Beautiful women wearing veils and lacy skirts, unclad from neck to hips. Peter looked on, interested, but with no desire to move. The women laughed and played in the pool. Every once in a while one of them would raise a slender arm and say a word, or perhaps a whole sentence, or just a syllable, and a peal of laughter would sweep the pool.

They're stoned, Peter realized after watching them for a while. *Not as bad as I was, but still tripped out.*

After several hours the men returned and carried Peter back to his little room. 'Here,' the same man demanded before he left, producing another glass, 'drink this!' The fluid was light blue this time. Peter again filled his mouth and again deposited it on the pillow when the men had gone. He tried to think about what was happening but fell asleep. His dreams were in bright splotches of color and filled with loud chords.

'Here, drink this!'

Peter came slowly awake and then snapped to full alertness as he realized what had happened. Did those under the influence of whatever that drug was go to sleep? He seemed to remember that hallucinogens kept their users awake for tremendous lengths of time.

The man holding the inevitable glass didn't seem concerned that he had found Peter asleep, so Peter decided not to worry about it. He took the glass with its small amount of fluid — again blue — and filled his mouth, then lay back, waiting for the man to leave.

'Come,' the man said, turning around and walking toward the door. Peter hastily spat the liquid onto the blanket and followed.

They walked down a maze of corridors, bare feet padding along the tile floor. The walls, of stone inlaid in places with tile, had a look of great age, and the doors they passed were masses of ancient wood. Peter kept his eyes forward, as though in drugged disinterest in all he passed. They turned left, and then left again, then right, then left, and stopped before one of the hewn wooden doorways. 'Enter,' the guide said.

Peter decided he had no choice, as resisting would give away the only edge he had, so he stepped through the door. He found himself in a cell-like room. The walls were of smooth, dark, seamless material, cold to the touch. His guide of few words didn't enter with him but closed the door from outside. The room was now pitch black, without even a gleam of light shining through the bottom of the door. Peter began to wonder if he should have run while he had the chance, but he had no idea where he could have run to. He decided his best bet was to keep them — whoever they were — thinking he was under the influence of the blue stuff in the glass. Actually the combined effects of the drug and tranquilizer had worn off in his sleep, and he felt weak but normal.

'Sit!' a voice commanded softly and without inflection. Peter sat on the floor.

'Who are you?' the voice asked. Peter tried to decide what he'd answer if he were still stoned. He decided that he'd think about it, and possibly giggle. He giggled. It pleased the voice.

'There is no you,' the voice told him. 'There is no you, you, you, you, you, you, you, you . . . ' It went on for some time, until the word had become a sound, and the sound a noise. If a word, any word, is repeated aloud often enough, it ceases to have any meaning. This works even for a normal person; for someone in a highly suggestible, drug-induced state, it works even better. Soon even the idea the word defines becomes meaningless.

' . . . you, you, you, you, you, you . . . ' The voice slowly faded off into silence, leaving Peter to think about it for a while.

'There is no I,' the voice resumed after a while, 'no I, I, I, I, I, I, I, I . . . ' It sounded like the chorus line of a Latin-American song. Peter wondered what the voice had against pronouns. Again the voice faded out.

'There is no self,' the voice proclaimed, and Peter was glad it was off pronouns. 'No self, self, self, self . . . ' Again it faded out, leaving him to think for a while. If this technique worked, Peter decided, he was glad he had no blue convincer sloshing around in his bloodstream.

The voice took up again with, 'There is no good, good, good, good . . . ' removing one more word from the dictionary. 'There is no evil, evil, evil, evil, evil . . . ' the voice exhorted evenly, settling an ancient point of religious dispute. It grew quiet again.

Slowly, and so subtly that at first Peter thought he was imagining it, a red illumination filled the cell, and weird shadows flickered across the walls. This time the voice started so softly it could barely be heard, and gradually grew until it reverberated from the walls, beating at his ears. 'There is only the will of Hasan, only the will of Hasan, only the will . . . ' The red light grew bright and changed to blue, yellow and green, at first slowly, and then with increasing speed until the colors blinked with the harsh intensity of strobe lights gone mad.

Peter started at the name, remembering the story of the assassins and their fanatic leader. But that was almost a thousand years ago — surely it couldn't . . . 'The will of Hasan, the will of Hasan . . . ' Perhaps it could.

It went on for hours, the words changing and becoming more exact as they drummed their ceaseless repetition into the unyielding walls of the small room. At first it was funny, and then boring, and then actually painful, as the sounds poured out in ceaseless, pounding rhythm. The lights kept blinking, weaving and changing; and the words kept pounding, pounding, pounding. Peter wanted to close his eyes and put his hands over his ears, but he was afraid he was being watched, so he sat in mindless wonder, gazing at the one-cell universe.

Peter was informed that he was to obey Hasan, that he was an instrument of Hasan, that he was a part of Hasan, that his actions were Hasan's will. It was a demand for a total, mindless obedience that has been accorded no tyrant, no prophet, no country and no church in all of human history. The consent of the governed had no more place in Hasan's scheme of things than the consent of the right hand is required to turn a switch or hold a knife. Peter wondered what form of chastisement was required for an erring servant. *If thy right hand offends thee*, he remembered, and stopped wondering.

Finally the symphony ended and blackness descended over the cell. 'You will be called,' was the voice's final comment. Peter remembered vaguely that the word 'you' had been stricken, but decided not to make an issue of it. He went to sleep.

★   ★   ★

The cell door opened. Its noise woke Peter at once, and he lay blinking at the unbearable light that came from the dim lamps in the corridor. A tall, slim, blond young man in the khaki dress Europeans regard as proper desert wear stood in the doorway. His face was bland and unlined, like a blackboard washed clear. 'Come,' he said.

Peter got up. 'Am I called?' he asked. The youth turned and started to walk away.

'Wait!' Peter said. The youth stopped. 'Where are we going?'

'To Hasan,' the youth said. There was a

251

trace of a British accent in the emotion-less voice, and Peter had a frightening suspicion.

'What's your name?' he asked, keeping in step with his companion's long strides.

There was no reply.

'Who are you?' Peter insisted. He hoped his questions were within the possibility of his new role and would cause no suspi-cion.

'I am the will of Hasan,' the youth answered. This was the longest sentence Peter had heard in days.

'Have you a name?'

No answer.

'What do you do?'

'What I am told.' There it was. Not even 'ordered' or 'commanded,' just 'told.' Not quite as good as a right hand, but close. You speak, he does. Not even 'obeys,' but performs as a logical consequence of your words. Like the bees in a hive danc-ing out their lives to the whim of a built-in instinct.

'Who were you?' Peter tried. Again no answer. It seemed to be a selective thing. Questions that made no sense to the new outlook simply weren't heard. Peter stopped trying.

They stopped before a large wooden door, and the youth opened it and stepped aside. 'Enter,' he said.

Peter did so, trying to match his companion's expressionless disinterest as befitted a new Instrument of Hasan. He almost failed immediately. The room was huge and magnificent, with the heavy-handed opulence of an Oriental potentate as dreamed of in Scheherazade's thousand-and-one nights of storytelling. The walls, such parts of them as blinked through the hanging tapestries, were frescoed with scenes from the legends of a part of the world that is the birthplace of legend. Unicorns peeked around corners here; there a satyr romped with veiled maidens. The hangings that interrupted the story line were rich with soft color and embroidered stories of their own. The chamber's furnishings were of heavy wood and rich fabric: a bed, tables, chairs, bureaus and lamps. They rested on a deep wide rug which had a scene of its own woven into three-dimensional life and traced with delicate colors.

Centered in the room, a few yards out from the massive bed, was a large table, its surface squared off by alternating slabs of black and white ivory, bearing two rows of half-foot-high black and white ivory chessmen, which were a few moves into their age-old battle. On one side of the table, shepherding the white pieces, sat a man, incredibly thin, unbelievably ancient, enveloped in a red satin robe, stroking the few long hairs of his beard and puffing on a pipe whose long and twisted stem terminated in a tiny ivory bowl. His chair was deep and bowed, its seat rising to a curved back and slender arms in the simple grace favored by the imperial Romans. Across from him, in a high-backed chair that would have graced the refectory of any medieval monastery, Professor Perlemutter sat as general of the black. His hands were tied behind the chair.

Peter's surprise, if it showed, was masked by the Professor's exclamation as he came into the room. 'Peter!' Perlemutter twisted around in his seat. 'How are you?'

Peter took his cue from the impassive youth at the door and didn't reply.

'Peter, can you hear me?'

'Yes,' Peter said flatly.

'It's as I told you, Professor,' the ancient said, his malevolent voice filling the room. He stood up and approached Peter, seeming to float across the floor. 'I am Hasan.' He held up his hands as if in some sort of benediction. 'Welcome! Welcome to the followers of Hasan.'

'Hasan,' Peter said, feeling that some sort of reply was called for. *If he asks me anything*, he thought, *I'm lost*. He felt pretty well lost anyway.

But the Old Man of the Mountain — or his present carnate self — requested nothing more of Peter. He stared at him a moment, his eyes gleaming with a dark glow that seemed able to read souls, then glided back to his seat. 'You see, Professor,' he said, his voice low and with the sibilant quality of a snake's warning, 'he is mine now. My creature and my tool.'

'Has he no will of his own?' Perlemutter asked, staring at Peter for a clue.

'None,' Hasan cackled. 'None. Oh, as time goes on the rigid quality will disappear, and he will be able to pass among his friends as quite normal. Perhaps a little lacking in imagination, but otherwise no change. But when I speak, or while in this place, his will is my will.' He raised one arm slightly, as though the gesture were a strain for him. 'Come,' he said, his voice deepening when he spoke to his servants, as an announcer's does when he addresses the camera eye of his audience. Peter recognized it as the voice that had been so recently drumming at him. He walked smoothly across the floor and stopped two paces from Hasan.

'I will have him move the chessmen for you, and you may observe him as he does. Since this was a close friend of yours, you will see how well my method works.' He gestured to Peter. 'Move the chessmen as Professor Perlemutter directs.' Then he turned to the door. 'Go get the woman,' he hissed. The young man standing in the doorway departed silently.

'It's his sister!' Perlemutter protested,

confirming Peter's guess.

'That will make no difference,' Hasan said confidently. 'If I can accomplish this with your friend Carthage in a week, do you doubt what I can do with this boy, who has been here several months?'

A week? Peter had no idea of the time that had passed, but he would have guessed much less — or, perhaps, remembering the eternity of hallucinations, much more. He wondered if Sara had been converted into a zombie.

'No,' Perlemutter said, 'I don't doubt it. Is that what you're going to do to me?'

'After you cease to amuse me,' Hasan said mildly. 'But you play a good game of chess; I may keep you around for a while. You don't have to worry for another week at least. I'm only set up to process one person at a time, and the woman is next.'

So she hadn't gone through the dream mill yet. Peter decided that it was about time to do something. He wondered if his body would, after all, obey him when he tried, or if this sense of free will was merely an illusion that all Hasan's servants had buried deep within them. It was a frightening thought.

'Does this system of yours always work?' Professor Perlemutter asked.

'No,' Hasan said. 'Not always. Although it is as far above the traditional methods as the drugs I use are above hashish, it has its failures. Luckily they're easily detectable. The very power that makes these modern potions so valuable proves too much for some sorts of minds. I will show you.' He reached out and rapped a small silver gong with a tiny mallet pulled from his robe. A soft ting raced across the room. In a second the great doors on the far side of the room had opened, and a pair of giants stood framed in the doorway like living versions of Gog and Magog. *Must watch out for that gong,* Peter thought.

'Go,' Hasan instructed, 'and bring me the one in the upper chamber.' Looking even in motion as though they'd been hewn from huge blocks of dark wood, the giant twins strode across the room and through the door Peter had entered.

'Can Peter answer when I speak to him?' the Professor asked.

'If you phrase the questions so they have relevance to him and I direct him to,' said Hasan. 'Others he will ignore. But let us now play chess; this conversation wearies me.'

Professor Perlemutter slumped in his chair as much as his tied hands would allow and glared at the board. He seemed to have given up hope. Peter could think of no way to reassure him that wouldn't give the game away.

'Pawn to king's bishop three,' Perlemutter said. Peter picked up the heavy pawn and moved it. He briefly thought of cracking Hasan over the head with it, but decided he'd better wait.

Hasan stared at the board for some time, obviously lost in the world of ivory men, and then with a quick, nervous gesture reached over and moved a knight. Then he leaned back and, with the slightest possible motion of his hand, put the pipe to his lips. He lit a taper from the lamp by his side and puffed at the glowing end. He seemed to do everything in sudden bursts of energy and be struck with incredible lassitude between the bursts.

When the thick, cloyingly sweet smell of the pipe reached Peter, he understood. Whatever drugs he gave his men, or used to create his mindless followers, he himself smoked opium.

The door opened and Gog and Magog entered, carrying between them a sack. They lowered the sack to the floor.

'Turn him around,' Hasan commanded. They did, and the sack became a man curled up in a tight ball, his head hidden by his legs. 'Straighten him out,' Hasan said.

They uncurled the body and lifted it up by the arms. It hung limply between them, its eyes open and staring, saliva dripping from its open mouth. The filthy remains of some sort of military uniform were draped around it.

'Allow me to introduce you to Captain Thor,' Hasan said, pointing a long, thin hand of scorn, 'late of the Desert Legion.'

Thor drooled.

'There was nothing inside of him but a large, frightened mass of identity problems,' Hasan said. 'And when the mind drug caused him to doubt, all the threads that held together his quivering psyche unraveled, leaving this.' He stood up and walked slowly over to his failure. His voice deepened, becoming gentle and powerful. So might the gods have spoken to man. 'Your name is Thor,' he said. 'You are Captain Thor of the Desert Legion. General Brontke needs you, Captain Thor; he relies on you. You are Captain Thor. Everyone knows and respects Captain Thor.' He went on like this, a compelling, hypnotic quality in his voice.

Peter could now understand the power in this frail man. His voice, possessing all the strength his body lacked, was a trained weapon: powerful, convincing, sincere, able to command all attention and convey any mood. It grabbed and held on with a strength far beyond that of the mere words it used as tools. You wanted to believe this man, to do as he asked. Men not under the influence of any drug could fall for the spell woven by this voice.

Thor followed Hasan with his eyes as the mystic droned the words of identity. His lips moved in a vacant smile, and he stopped drooling. The words were reassuring, and the voice was commanding.

Peter felt badly shaken. In his ears there was an undertone, faintly heard beneath the magic voice. A breath of evil riding a sweetly scented wind. There was the vague feeling of horrid corruption and decay.

The almost tangible flow of words braced Thor, and he stood by himself, a faint intelligence coming into his eyes. Hasan paused and pointed his long hand. 'Captain Thor!' he suddenly barked. 'Attenshun!'

Thor snapped to attention, feet together, hands at his sides, his face rigid.

Hasan, hands clasped behind him, paced back and forth in front of Thor in a superb parody of the military manner: 'Captain Thor, I am going to entrust you with an important assignment.'

'Yes, sir,' Thor said smartly.

'It involves danger, Captain Thor, but because you are Captain Thor, I'm depending on you. You are Captain Thor and I'm depending on you. Captain Thor is needed. Is that clear?'

'Yes, sir.'

'Good, Captain Thor. An aide will come in with the message I want you to deliver in just a moment. Stand there until I call you.'

'Yes, sir.' Thor saluted.

Hasan returned the salute sharply. 'Very good.' He turned and, casting off the assumed military bearing like a discarded puppet, glided back to his chair.

Professor Perlemutter stared. 'I've never seen, I've never heard of anyone able to treat catatonia like that,' he said.

'Yes,' Hasan said. 'A parlor trick to amuse psychologists. But I'm afraid it's only a trick.

As they watched, Captain Thor's hands loosened slackly at his sides, his face relaxed, and his mouth crept open.

'I don't really consider the military face any more intelligent,' Hasan commented, 'but at least it's able to obey orders.'

Thor's eyes lost interest, and his body slowly folded over like a collapsing folding chair until he was again in a fetal position on the floor.

Hasan waved at the twin wooden

giants. 'Take him away and go back to your places.' They picked up the sack and carted it out of the room.

'What are you going to do with him?' Perlemutter asked.

'Most of them I destroy,' Hasan said calmly, 'but a few I keep until I can find a cure. It might happen to someone I need sometime.'

'You destroy?' Professor Perlemutter sounded shocked for the first time since Peter had known him.

'Yes. They're a lot of trouble to take care of. Let us continue the chess game.'

Hasan returned his attention to the game, but Perlemutter kept staring at him. 'What do you hope to gain from this?' he asked. 'Are you setting up to, er, follow in the footsteps of your eleventh-century predecessor?'

Hasan curled up in his chair and cackled, looking suddenly like a shriveled-up old gnome. 'You mean assassination? Killing, as my American friends would have it, for fun and profit? No, not at all. That was fine in the time of the Byzantine Empire, but other methods, other goals.'

He straightened out again, and leaned forward. 'I mean to control the world,' he said in a high, thin whisper.

The Professor mumbled something to himself. Hasan leaned forward. 'What was that?'

'I said you're mad!' Perlemutter snapped.

The Old Man of the Mountain stared at him for some time before he replied. 'That may be, but my methods aren't. When all the key men in the governments and opinion-making bodies of the world powers are 'hands' of Hasan — ' He thrust his own bony hands forward as example. ' — then the real power in the world will most assuredly be mine.'

Professor Perlemutter thought about that for a second. 'I understand,' he said. 'You haven't been trying to assassinate these people, but take them prisoner.'

'Quite so,' Hasan assented.

'Even those attempts on the Sheik of Jeppet. They seemed like bungled attempts at assassination, but they were never intended for that.'

'True,' Hasan agreed. 'It's so much harder merely to kidnap someone instead of killing him. But Al-Rashid dead does me no good at all, while Al-Rashid under my control is worth one-seventh of the world's supply of oil. The harder task is worth the greatest gain, as always.'

The Hand of Hasan that had been Quinline came through the door, escorting a woman whom he no longer recognized as his sister. Her hands were tied behind her back and her mouth was covered with a wide band of adhesive tape. 'The woman,' he announced.

'Very good,' Hasan said. 'Wait outside.' Quinline turned and left, closing the door behind him.

Sara walked slowly across the room, her eyes darting from one person to another, trying hard to understand the tableau before her.

Hasan turned to Peter. 'Remove the tape from her mouth,' he ordered.

It's time, Peter decided. *Now or never, as they say in the old war movies.* He walked over to Sara and gently pulled the tape from her mouth.

'What — ' she started.

Peter whirled and kicked sideways,

knocking Hasan's chair away from the gong. The chair tipped over, spilling Hasan onto the thick carpet. For a moment he lay there, stunned and surprised; but then, quick as a cat, he sprang up and dove for the gong. Peter grabbed him, knocked him down and held him on the floor. Hasan twisted over, breaking out of Peter's grip with surprising strength, and opened his mouth to yell. Peter rolled and punched him in the stomach, knocking the air out of his lungs, then grabbed his skinny arms and twisted them behind his back. Rolling him over onto his side, Peter slapped the piece of tape over his mouth, then took the belt from his robe and quickly tied his hands behind his back.

'There, that should do for now,' Peter said, standing up and dusting himself off. Hasan lay rigidly on the carpet, glaring his hatred up at Peter.

'My good lord,' Professor Perlemutter said, 'I thought you were Hasan's zombie.'

'So did he,' Peter said. 'Let me get those ropes off your arms and transfer them to the old one's legs.'

'A splendid idea,' Perlemutter agreed.

'Carthage comes through again. You must tell me about it sometime.'

'Right,' Peter agreed. 'Sometime in the very near future, but not now. We're in a hurry.' He bent down to work on the knotted cords.

'What's happening here?' Sara was backed up against one of the posts of the large bed, staring from one of them to the other. 'My brother's gone mad, I've been locked in a room for a week, and now this.'

'It's a bit complicated,' Peter told her. He finished tying up Hasan's legs with the rope from the Professor's wrists. 'Let's get out of here first, and I'll try to explain.'

'Let's get out of here, and I'll wait for the explanation.'

'We're agreed,' Peter said, untying her arms. 'First thing is to get this one out of sight.' He picked up Hasan and dumped him on the bed, drawing the thick curtains closed.

'You have a plan to get us out of here?' Perlemutter asked.

'Boldness, speed and luck,' Peter said. 'Let's get going.'

'Wait one second,' the Professor said. He inspected the chessboard and moved one of his bishops. 'Check!'

'Your brother's in a sort of hypnotic trance,' Peter told Sara. 'We'll take him with us if we can, but don't speak to him until we get out.'

'If you say so,' Sara agreed reluctantly.

Peter opened the door. Quinline was still waiting outside. 'Is the car we came in still here?' Peter asked him.

'Yes,' Quinline said.

'Take us to it.'

Quinline turned around and started walking. There was a sudden commotion from behind the bed curtains, but Quinline didn't notice. Peter pulled the doors shut behind him.

At a slow, deliberate pace that Peter was afraid to rush, Quinline led the procession down the long corridors. 'Hasan will get to that gong pretty quickly,' Perlemutter whispered. 'He'll bang it with his head if he has to.'

'I'm afraid so,' Peter whispered back. 'I should have tied him to the bed, but it's too late now. Know any effective prayers?'

269

A steep stone staircase dropped away to the right and twisted quickly out of sight. Quinline entered it and started descending, with the others following closely behind. They circled around and around in a rapidly descending spiral.

'Do you hear something?' Perlemutter whispered.

Peter made out the heavy stamp of footsteps above them. 'I believe I do.' As they rounded another corner, he spotted a niche carved into the rock above him. 'Let's see if I can get up there.'

Perlemutter boosted him up, and he was just able to get the tips of his fingers over the ledge. He pulled himself up into the narrow slot. 'Keep going. I'll try some sort of delaying action.'

Sara looked as though she were about to argue, but Perlemutter pushed her forward, and they disappeared down the stairs.

In a very few seconds the footsteps had grown louder, and then one of Hasan's giant guards appeared. *Tweedledum*, Peter thought. The other came right behind. *And Tweedledee.*

In perfect step they thundered past the ledge Peter was snuggled into without seeing him. As the second head passed slightly below him, Peter dropped from the ledge and kicked as he fell. His bare heels caught the second giant right behind the ear. He careened forward, crashing into the other, and they both went tumbling down the steep staircase. *Agreed to have a battle.*

Landing on his feet in approved karate fashion, Peter ran down the stone steps. He came upon the two guards lying in a heap on the second landing below the ledge. 'Pardon me,' Peter said, stepping on the first stomach; 'excuse me, please,' treading on the second chest. Then he continued running.

He caught up with the group at the bottom of the stairway. 'All clear,' he said.

'You're out of breath,' Perlemutter observed.

'I don't get enough exercise,' Peter agreed.

They walked down another corridor and came out into a small courtyard. At the far end, by a low stone wall, two men stood guarding a wooden winch-like affair with a large straw basket at the end of the rope. Trying to look as though he belonged and knew what he was doing, Peter walked with Quinline over to the edge of the stone wall. Looking over, he saw that the wall was a sheer drop of almost a hundred feet on the other side. There was a narrow trail below.

'Where's the car?' Peter asked.

'Behind that rock,' Quinline said, pointing across the trail.

'Let's get to it. How do we get down?'

'In the basket.' Quinlin walked over to the primitive elevator. 'Lower us down,' he said to one of the men. They looked at him blankly. He made a gesture of swinging the wooden boom over the side and operating the huge crank. One of the men nodded.

'Wait a second,' Peter said. He strode over to where Sara and Professor Perlemutter were waiting in the doorway. 'Let's go.'

'Look at this first,' Perlemutter said, pointing to a door set in the wall. Peter looked inside. The small, dank stone room held racks and racks of swords and spears. In a far corner there were even a few crossbows.

'No guns,' Peter said. 'Pity, but we'll have to make do.' He picked out one of the swords, a heavy-handled scimitar with a broad blade and razor-sharp edge, and stuck it carefully in his belt. Then the three of them walked across the courtyard.

The guards took no notice of Peter's weapon, but they objected when the four escapees tried to climb into the basket. One of them shook his head sharply and held up two fingers.

'Problem,' Professor Perlemutter said. 'We'll have to leave in sections.'

'You and Sara go first,' Peter decided. 'We'll follow.'

The Professor climbed into the straw lift, followed by Sara. The two men swung the boom out over the wall and slowly cranked the massive handle. Inch by inch, taking, it seemed to Peter, several hours, the basket approached the ground. Then finally they were down, and the men quickly cranked the basket back up.

'Come,' Peter said, and Quinline climbed into the basket with him without argument.

For the second time the basket crept down the wall, swinging gently from side to side and scraping against the stones. The ground ever so gradually came up to meet them. Suddenly there was a commotion from above, voices yelling things Peter couldn't understand. The basket stopped twelve feet off the ground and then slowly started to move up again. A face appeared over the parapet and yelled down something.

Quinine looked up mutely.

'Stop them!' the face commanded in English.

Quinine jerked back as if struck and then made a dive for Peter. Peter yanked the sword out of his belt and struck Quinine a sharp blow on the head with the hilt. Then he started hacking savagely at the rope that held the basket as Quinline fell in a heap at his feet. After a few agonizing seconds, during which the basket kept crawling back up the wall, the rope gave, and the basket, with a sickening lurch, fell the twelve feet to the ground. Peter dove forward out of the basket and rolled to his feet. He dragged Quinline out of the overturned basket and lifted him to his shoulders.

'Over here!' Sara called.

Peter ran across the narrow trail toward where she was standing. Something sharp sliced into his arm and clattered to the ground. He glanced up just in time to dodge a second spear hurled by one of the men on the wall. More spears were falling, and a sharp twanging sound told him that at least one of the men was using a crossbow. He couldn't see where the quarrel went.

'Here, in here.' Sara led the way through a narrow cleft in the rocks to where the car sat in a small cave. Perlemutter was behind the wheel, and the motor was running.

'How do we get out of here?' the Professor asked.

'They got in,' Peter said. He slung Quinline into the back seat and went over to inspect the massive rock in front of the car. There was a steel rod set into one side of it. Peter tugged on the rod and nothing happened. Then he pushed it. The rock slid aside as smoothly as a safe door opening. 'Let's go,' he yelled, jumping into the front seat. The Professor gunned the engine and raced the car through the narrow gap onto the road.

They careened down the trail away from the fortress for some time before anyone spoke. Then Sara touched Peter's shoulder. 'Your arm is bleeding.'

'Funny about that,' Peter said, and he held still while she wrapped a bandage around it.

16

Looking to the scout plane circling high above like a group of toy tanks squared off for battle in a sandbox, the Desert Legion prepared to roll. All the tents had been struck, holes had been covered in, and sand had been swept over sand with true military efficiency.

From ground level in front of the column, where Lieutenant Khazar stood with his general, all resemblance to toys vanished. The sixty-ton monsters surrounding him made the ground shake with their presence even when they were motionless and their powerful engines only idled.

General Brontke crouched in the sand by one of his ninety-ton Tigers. His ear was fixed to the speaker of an all-band radio perched beside him. The radio's twelve-foot whip antenna nodded of its own inertia in the breezeless air, punctuating the silence of the group of men surrounding Brontke. The clipped British accents of the announcer sounded small against the muted throbs of the many diesels in the background.

' . . . And this concludes our special broadcast of the transference of sovereignty from the British governor, Sir Cecil Piphes, as the official representative of Her Majesty, to the Sheik and the people of Jeppet. Since the last contingent of British troops and administrative personnel left yesterday, this ceremony marks the final step in the process of creating an independent Jeppet. With British stewardship at an end and Jeppet now ready to take her rightful place in the Commonwealth, the symbolic importance of . . . '

With an impatient twist of his wrist, General Brontke turned off the receiver. 'It is done,' he said to no one in particular. 'Jeppet is now independent; the British can no longer take an interest in its affairs, and we are ready to roll. We must give them no more time to prepare. We strike now!' He stood up and straightened the crease in his trousers. 'You're ready?' he asked Colonel Bahar.

'We will start out at your command,' Bahar assured Brontke.

'Good. Your trucks should arrive at the rendezvous point as much as an hour ahead of the tanks since you will be traveling on paved road, even though our route is straighter. I'll expect you to have all the fuel drums unloaded and ready to start refueling as soon as we arrive.'

'Yes, sir,' Bahar said. 'I anticipate no trouble.'

'Neither do I,' Brontke said, fixing a stern eye on his second-in-command. 'Neither do I. Move out!'

'Yes, sir.' Bahar gave a sharp salute, which was returned by Brontke. The colonel turned and double-timed across the sand with his officers following. Brontke gestured, and the rest of the men scattered to their vehicles.

Commander-General Brontke climbed stiffly into the lead tank and waited motionlessly while the line of trucks and armored cars roared into motion. Lieutenant Khazar strapped the bulky receiver to the rear of the tank and clambered through the hatch to his own position as radioman. He ran a quick communications cheek with the other tanks and then reported to Brontke. 'All ready, General.'

Brontke looked overhead to where the observation plane was being erratically piloted by an ill-trained lieutenant. 'I wonder what did happen to Captain Thor,' he mused; then he flipped the switch on his general communications microphone. 'Tanks for-r-ward!' he yelled, with an accompanying hand signal for any who might be in doubt.

The throbbing rose to a high, grinding whine, and the Desert Legion, secret force of a mighty Arab power, rolled to the attack.

17

Tony Ryan switched off his shortwave radio and turned to Mondar. 'The trucks are coming now. It's your show.'

Mondar bowed slightly. 'We're ready.'

'Fine. Just consider me an observer. I'll watch from behind the roadblock.' Tony clambered over the logs and stationed himself behind the barrier next to the three men working the recoilless rifle.

★   ★   ★

Up the road about three miles away, the convoy of trucks slowly maneuvered around the narrow turns. Colonel Bahar stood with his body half out of the hatch in the leading armored car, staring up at the cliffs to his left.

'This would be an altogether excellent spot for an ambush,' he said.

'This whole damn road,' the machine gunner standing next to him added, 'would be a damned good spot for an ambush.'

'I didn't ask you.' Bahar tightened the strap of his helmet and looked firmly ahead. 'You stick to your gun.' He stuck his head back inside the car. 'Driver! Speed it up.'

'Right, sir,' the driver said. The armored car lurched forward.

'Watch out for the cliff,' Bahar yelled as the drop on the right came dangerously close.

'Yes, sir.'

'Slow down again.'

The driver sighed quietly. 'Right, sir.'

The column followed the highway as it dropped from its mountain heights back down to the valley below. As it progressed, the highway grew broader, and Bahar became less worried.

'We're almost there.'

'Yes,' the gunner agreed. 'Yes, sir. Just a short way now.'

★ ★ ★

Tony was pacing back and forth in the narrow strip of road behind the barricade.

'Get the armored car in the lead, and the trucks behind it will be fine stationary targets for your men up in the rocks,' he said to Mondar.

'As we discussed,' Mondar agreed. 'And we will get the last truck to cut off their retreat. It's all planned.'

'Right,' Tony said. 'Sorry.' He sat down. The low engine noise of the trucks was now quite clear and growing louder.

The armored car came into view around the curve. Two men were standing in the opened hatch. They saw the pile of timber in front of them and dove into the vehicle, slamming the cover closed on top of them. The car came steadily forward. Behind it the first and then the second truck came into view. The machine gun in the armored car's turret started burping, and steel-jacketed bullets whined over the head of the men crouched behind the barricade and gouged into the logs, sending up a spray of wood chips.

'Hold fire,' Mondar instructed his gunners kneeling by the long snout of the recoilless rifle. 'Let it get closer. Wait — Wait — Now!'

The rifle coughed, and an arc of fire cut into the sky. The arc passed just over the armored car, rose slightly and dropped on the second truck, which gave a crunching sound and blossomed into flame.

The armored car kept coming, chattering death from two machine guns. One was placed too low to do more than eat wood out of the barricade, but the slugs from the other came closer. They dug into the dirt behind them as the gunners struggled to lower the aim of the rifle, which was resting firmly on a log of the barricade. One of the gunners suddenly jerked up and fell backward away from the gun. His chest turned red, and a look of surprise froze on his face as he lay still beneath the hot sun.

Mondar jumped to take the man's place, and the crew finished twisting the gun down to a lower sighting. By this time the car was almost at the barrier, and bullets were hitting all around them.

'Now!' Mondar yelled.

The firer reached out for the trigger and then looked down at his leg, where a wood splinter was protruding through a large hole in the fleshy part of his thigh, and fell silently to the ground. The car started to push into the timber of the barricade.

Tony dove for the trigger and squeezed. A tremendous roar echoed off the steel plates as the anti-tank round pierced the shell of the car at point-blank range. The armored car shuddered, lifted into the air and fell back with a grinding lurch. A second later there was another roar, and the armored car blew into pieces like a giant hand grenade. The force of the blast knocked Tony to the ground. A large chunk of metal bedded itself deeply into the earth only inches away from his head.

For a long moment Tony lay there, stunned. When his senses returned, he gingerly sat up and felt the back of his neck. 'I think I've got what they call whiplash,' he said to the surrounding air. 'My neck feels like it no longer has any interest in holding up my head.' He got up and stood still for a moment while an attack of dizziness passed and then walked over to where Mondar was squatting on the road, wrapping a long white bandage around the neck and chin of the last member of the gun crew. Both of Mondar's hands were soaked with blood. 'How is he?' Tony asked.

'A small piece of metal seems to have cut through here and there,' Mondar said, indicating the right side of the neck and chin. 'It's a clean wound; he should be all right.'

'Good,' Tony said. 'And how are you?'

Mondar held up his right hand in answer. Tony saw that not all the blood was from the other man. There was a hole the size of a quarter through Mondar's palm. 'A small price,' he said.

'Perhaps,' Tony agreed, marveling that Mondar could still manipulate the hand with a wound that had severed the muscles to the fingers and must be causing intense pain. 'But let's do something about it.' He finished wrapping the gunner's wound for Mondar, tied it off, and then applied a length of sterile bandage to Mondar's hand. Then he broke out two one-shot syringes of morphine from his medical kit and applied them to the upper arm muscles of each of his patients.

'Thank you,' Mondar said, fashioning a sling for his arm and standing up. 'This should do. What's happening?'

'I'll see,' Tony said. He scrambled to the top of the barricade. The armored car had all but disappeared, with only a mass of twisted, unidentifiable metal leaning against the barrier. The three trucks in view behind it were all burning. A scattering of men in the uniform of the Desert Legion stood in small groups in the road, with their hands on their heads, looking bewildered. The Quarati soldiers were climbing down the cliff face from their ambush position to take charge of the prisoners. One change they had made when they switched from warriors to soldiers was that now they had to take prisoners.

'It looks like it's all over,' Tony said. 'Let's go see.' With Tony's help, Mondar made his way over the logjam, and they started down the road. When the rest of the convoy came into view around the curve, the sight was much the same. It looked more impressive from here, as the burning column of trucks seemed to cast a pall of black smoke as far back as the eye could make out. The armored cars, stuck behind every fourth truck, were uninjured, but their crews, realizing their helpless position, were deserting them and lining up with other legionnaires.

One of the nearby trucks gave a deep bellow, and a pool of oil started settling across the road. The bright flame reached the pool and raced across the road on the surface of the oil, blocking the road from side to side. The intense wave of heat drove back the men near the truck.

'The drums are bursting!' Tony yelled over the sound of burning. 'We'd better get everyone away from here fast — pretty soon this whole area is going to be a lake of burning oil!'

The men of el Quarat and their prisoners gathered up the road on the far side of the blockade. They stood staring at the black smoke enveloping the side of the mountain.

'It's amazing what a few bottles filled with gasoline can do,' Mondar observed.

'Right,' Tony said. 'The Molotov

cocktail is a fearsome weapon, given the right conditions. We'd better get out of here before Brontke and his tanks arrive.'

'Our job is done,' Mondar agreed.

18

The tanks of the Desert Legion approached the rendezvous point, and General Brontke became aware of a thick haze that obscured the mountains to the left. As they grew nearer, and Brontke could make out the dense clouds of black smoke that billowed up to make the haze, a suspicion formed in his mind. He waved one of the support cars forward. 'Go investigate that smoke, and report back immediately,' he told the driver. The light armored car dashed off to the left. 'If that's what I think it is,' Brontke growled, 'I'm going to have that Bahar court-martialed.'

Lieutenant Khazar, his head stuck out of the hatch beside Brontke, had already formed his own idea of what the smoke was. 'Supposing Bahar's dead?' he asked without thinking.

'Then I'll conduct his court-martial posthumously,' Brontke stated flatly. Khazar could think of no reply.

The tanks grumbled on until they reached the point of rendezvous. There were no trucks waiting for them with neatly unloaded barrels of diesel oil waiting to refuel the steel juggernauts. Brontke was surprisingly calm as he ordered the drivers to shut off their engines.

Ten minutes later the scout car came careening back down the road. It reached the lead tank, braked to a stop, and the driver jumped out. 'Sir, the trucks have been destroyed,' he nervously told Brontke.

'All of them?'

'Yes, sir. I couldn't even get close to them, the heat was so high.'

'Very well,' Brontke said, dismissing the driver. He leaned down and spoke to his driver, whose head was sticking out of the forward hatch. 'How much fuel do we have left?'

The driver checked hurriedly. 'Slightly under half full,' he reported.

'Ha!' Brontke exclaimed. 'With that and the few barrels of oil strapped to the backs of the tanks not carrying other supplies, we should be able to fill just about half of the tanks. We'll start siphoning procedures immediately.' He watched impatiently as tank after tank had the long rubber siphon inserted into its fuel tank, and the precious black liquid ran into empty drums to be hand-pumped to other tanks.

When the job was completed, there were twenty-two tanks full of fuel and ready to continue. 'Use the oil left in your tanks to form a circle,' Brontke told the commanders of the tanks to be left behind. 'Stay in a defensive posture until we return. With twenty-two tanks we'll still have no trouble against the fourteen in the untrained Army of Jeppet. After the first battle, we shall be secure. After all, what is Jeppet but a vast oil dump? We go on!'

The twilight deepened as Brontke guided his reduced but still very powerful Desert Legion toward its destiny.

19

The command post of the Jeppet forces stood on a sand-free hill poking out of the surrounding desert. In front of it stretched the great barren wasteland. Behind it, the cliffs that made up the coastline climbed gradually, to drop suddenly away to the city of Akr and the Persian Gulf.

'That's that,' Peter said to the group gathered around him inside the command tent. He took off his earphones. 'Brontke's observation plane has landed by the circle of fuelless tanks, probably also out of fuel. Tony thinks the men left behind will be glad to surrender after a few days of rationed water, and I agree. So our only worry is the force headed toward us.'

'But that's still quite a force,' ben Dulli said. 'The first part of your scheme worked nicely, but we still face a tank group one-third larger than our own. The remainder of your plan had better also work.'

'Have faith,' Peter said, smiling. 'And get some sleep if you can; the legion won't reach us before dawn tomorrow.'

The group scattered to take Peter's advice, and he decided to try it himself. He climbed into his sleeping bag, snuggled down and started to worry. After a time the worries merged into dreams, and he fell asleep. Not all the dreams were good.

It seemed only a few minutes later when he woke to the deep throbbing of tank engines. Hurriedly putting on his boots, he rushed out into the dark. 'What's happening?' he asked a dim figure standing on the rise overlooking the parked tanks.

'It's almost dawn,' the figure answered in Professor Perlemutter's voice. 'I was going to wake you in a few minutes. Our advance scouts report the legion about fifteen miles away.'

'That's damn close,' Peter said. 'I don't want these boys trying our maneuvers in the dark.'

'They won't be,' Professor Perlemutter assured him. 'My trusty almanac puts dawn about six minutes away.'

'Very good. And the sun will be glaring in the collective eyes of the legion. That's good, too.'

'Yes,' Perlemutter agreed. 'Come have some coffee.'

'What, no last-minute words of encouragement to the troops?'

'I took care of that,' said Perlemutter. 'As the tank crews left the briefing tent, I solemnly intoned, 'Jeppet expects every man to do his duty.' Will that do?'

'Derivative, but adequate,' Peter said, allowing himself to be led into the command tent.

'Sorry, it's the best I could do at five in the morning.'

A cup of coffee was thrust at Peter as he entered the tent. He took it and gulped down some of the too-hot liquid. 'You could have tried, 'We have raised a banner in the sight of all good men and true. The event is in the hands of God.''

'Not bad,' Perlemutter approved. 'Who said it, Martin Luther or Oliver Cromwell?'

'George Washington said something

like it,' Peter said. He bent over the radio operator. 'What's happening?'

The operator looked up. 'The legion's about twelve miles away now. Nothing to do but wait.'

Peter walked outside as the first light of the coming day broke over the hills. The waiting was the hard part. He sat on a rock and slowly sipped his coffee. The tanks, all fourteen of them, were out of sight now, churning up the desert somewhere between here and the legion.

About fifteen minutes later, as Peter was finishing his coffee, the sound of tank guns — a distant, hollow noise — was carried back to him on the cool morning air. The battle was on.

The sun rose, and the light brightened into full day as the sounds of fighting grew closer. Then the Jeppet tanks appeared as tiny clouds of dust in the distance. Spread out across the sand, they were racing in full retreat into the horseshoe formed by the surrounding hills. Peter counted them as they came and stopped at nine. 'Five gone already,' he muttered.

'Here comes the legion,' ben Dulli announced, and Peter first noticed him standing on a rock with a pair of binoculars to his eyes.

Peter stared into the dust storm created by the fleeing Jeppet tanks until he thought his eyes would burn out. He could just make out the hulking shapes in close pursuit.

'What in the name of Allah are those?' ben Dulli demanded, staring at the approaching horde.

Peter grabbed his own binoculars and stood up. At first he could see nothing but sand, but then the distant tanks came into focus. At the lead, in front of the Desert Legion's forces, were four giant tanks Peter couldn't identify. He handed his binoculars to Professor Perlemutter. 'You ever see anything like those before?'

Perlemutter squinted off into the distance. 'They're Tigers,' he said after a moment. 'World War Two German stuff. Biggest tanks ever made. I wonder where Brontke got them.'

'Can we take them?' Peter demanded.

'I should think so. They're obsolete,

twenty years out of date. No trouble. If it was just our tanks we couldn't even hole them. But,' he added with a tight smile, 'our secret weapon is better than their secret weapon.'

'That's a relief.' Now Jeppet's forces were almost to the far end of the valley, parallel with the command post, and all the Desert Legion's tanks had entered the horseshoe. The ground reverberated with the roar of wheeling tanks and the boom of heavy-caliber guns. Jeppet's tanks started climbing the sand-dune ridge at the far end of the valley.

One of the rear tanks was passing right below the command point, its turret twisted to the rear and its gun firing round after round at the approaching legion vehicles. Suddenly it spun around from a direct hit, its left tread spilling off the rollers like a striking snake. Immobile below them, with smoke threading up from the rear, it continued firing into the oncoming mass of armor.

One of the legion tanks came racing toward it, firing as it came. It scored another direct hit and wheeled away as the Jeppet tank settled, with a burping sound, into the sand. The hatches flew open and five men dove out and scattered. The jacket of one of the men was on fire, and he rolled in the sand to put it out. Then the tank blew up and, in a few seconds, was enveloped by flames.

'Those,' Peter said, 'are good men, well trained or not.' Ben Dulli nodded agreement but was speechless.

The last Jeppet tank climbed the hill, and the mass of legion armor gathered below them. 'It's time,' Peter said. Ben Dulli pulled a flare gun from his belt and fired. A bright red signal flare burst over the valley.

On the crest of the hills, widely spaced along the horseshoe, squat, angular vehicles appeared. Steel-plated, with two metal arms bent behind them, they looked like a cross between a small armored car and a mechanical grasshopper. Each of the arms clutched a stubby, finned rocket.

'The crucial moment is at hand,' Peter said. 'If Brontke's boys manage to stick together and blast through the center, they've won the battle. But if we can break them up, it's all over.'

A rocket on one of the cars flamed and spurted forward in a flat arc. It moved with a slow, stubby, majestic dignity through the air, then curved down and to the left, intersecting with one of the legion's tanks. There was a dull thump. Another rocket took to the air.

Brontke's tanks swiveled to fire at these new targets, but the tank destroyers were above them and at extreme range for their guns. The shells fell with no effect. In a collective convulsive movement, the legion tanks started separating, each commander trying to close in on the nearest rocket car. Slowly and deliberately, one at a time, the rockets continued firing. The scene broke into a free-for-all of individual tank actions.

The Jeppet armored force, which had disappeared over the rise to the front, made its way around the ring of dunes and now appeared in the entrance to the horseshoe, keeping the legion tanks bottled up in the valley.

If they had stuck together, the mass of

legion tanks could have broken out in any direction, but the force had been effectively broken up. Jamming equipment being run by the radio operator in the command tent kept Brontke from communicating any orders to his commanders. Each commander now considered himself on his own, and separately they were trapped.

The fighting continued for a few minutes, with one of the legion tanks actually getting close enough to an armored rocket car to put a round in it before another rocket took it out. Then the futility of individual action became apparent to one of the Desert Legion commanders. He stopped his vehicle and raised the top hatch, coming out onto the turret with his hands up. In a form of chain reaction, the other legion tanks ground one by one to a stop and threw their hatches open.

In a short space of time all the remaining legion forces had surrendered, with one exception. The lead tank, a Tiger, kept grinding its way up the hill, its gun firing, until a final rocket stopped it by knocking off a tread.

Peter sat back down on his rock and let

out his breath. He wondered how long he'd been holding it. 'It worked,' he said.

'Divide and conquer, a principle that antedates Alexander the Great,' Professor Perlemutter said, sounding satisfied.

The hatch on the disabled Tiger opened, and a tall figure clambered out and climbed down to the ground. He was waving and seemed to be yelling something. He tried to continue in the direction his tank had been going — up the hill — but slid down the loose sand as fast as he climbed. Another man climbed out of the hatch and started after him but then shrugged and sat down on the turret.

'Look at that,' ben Dulli said, pointing at the scene.

Peter focused his binoculars. 'That red line down the trouser leg makes him a general officer in those old Wehrmacht uniforms,' he said. 'It must be Brontke.'

The general fell down to his hands and knees and started to crawl up the hill. He was pushing a small object in front of him.

'Can you make out what he has there?' ben Dulli asked.

Peter studied the thing General Brontke was pushing. 'It looks to me like a toy tank.'

They watched in silence while the surrendered remnants of the Desert Legion attack force were gathered together and General Pertival Hals Von-und-Zu Brontke kept trying to push his toy tank up to the crest of the hill.

20

The last of the search party clambered down the scaling ladders to the trail below, and the captain in charge walked over to the jeep where Peter sat with his arm around Sara. 'It's as you thought,' he said. 'The place is empty, not even a stick of furniture left behind.'

Peter nodded. 'I thought Hasan would have other bolt-holes.'

'Gone but not forgotten,' Sara said. 'My brother won't get out of the hospital for several months yet. Did Hasan really think he could take over Jeppet?'

'He was so convinced that he tried to destroy Brontke's tanks so they couldn't beat him to it. He was after more than Jeppet.'

Sara shuddered. 'I'm glad we've seen the last of him.'

'Have we?' Peter said. 'I wonder.'

The captain saluted. 'We have to be getting back to Akr,' he said. 'Will you be coming with us?'

'No.' Peter smiled. 'We're the expected guests of Sherif el Quarat. We'll be there for a few nights, I expect.'

Sara hugged him, and he put the jeep in gear and started off down the trail. Soon they were lost from sight.

We do hope that you have enjoyed reading this large print book.

Did you know that all of our titles are available for purchase?

We publish a wide range of high quality large print books including:
Romances, Mysteries, Classics
General Fiction
Non Fiction and Westerns

Special interest titles available in large print are:
The Little Oxford Dictionary
Music Book, Song Book
Hymn Book, Service Book

Also available from us courtesy of Oxford University Press:
Young Readers' Dictionary
(large print edition)
Young Readers' Thesaurus
(large print edition)

For further information or a free brochure, please contact us at:
Ulverscroft Large Print Books Ltd.,
The Green, Bradgate Road, Anstey,
Leicester, LE7 7FU, England.
Tel: (00 44) **0116 236 4325**
Fax: (00 44) **0116 234 0205**

A QUESTION OF GUILT

Tony Gleeson

Dane Spilwell, a brilliant surgeon, stands accused of the brutal murder of his wife. The evidence against him is damning, his guilt almost a foregone conclusion. Two red-haired women will determine his ultimate fate. One, a mysterious lady in emeralds, may be the key to clearing him of the crime — if only she can be located. The other, Detective Jilly Garvey, began by doggedly working to convict him — but now finds herself doubting his culpability . . .

TWEAK THE DEVIL'S NOSE

Richard Deming

Driving to the El Patio club to see his girlfriend Fausta Moreni, the establishment's proprietor, private investigator Manville Moon does not expect to be witness to a murder. As he steps from his car outside the club, he hears a gun suddenly roar from the bushes close behind him. Walter Lancaster, the lieutenant governor of the neighbouring state of Illinois, has been shot! The assassination will not only make headlines all over the country, but also place the lives of Moon and Fausta in deadly danger . . .

THE MAN WITH THE CAMERA EYES

Victor Rousseau

Investigative lawyer Langton has solved many bizarre cases with the help of his friend Peter Crewe, who possesses such an extraordinary photographic memory that he never forgets a face. Here Langton relates twelve stories featuring audacious jewel robberies, scientific geniuses gone mad and bad, and cold-blooded murder served up via amusement park rides, craftily concealed explosives, and hot air balloons. In each, the Man with the Camera Eyes provides the observations and deductions that are crucial to the solution of the mystery — often risking his own life in the process . . .

THE SEPIA SIREN KILLER

Richard A. Lupoff

Prior to World War II, black actors were restricted to minor roles in mainstream films — though there was a 'black' Hollywood that created films with all-black casts for exhibition to black audiences. When a cache of long-lost films is discovered by cinema researchers, the aged director Edward 'Speedy' MacReedy appears to reclaim his place in film history. But insurance investigator Hobart Lindsey and homicide officer Marvia Plum soon find themselves enmeshed in a frightening web of arson and murder with its roots deep in the tragic events of a past era . . .

KILLING COUSINS

Fletcher Flora

Suburban housewife Willie Hogan is selfish, bored, and beautiful, passing her time at the country club and having casual affairs. Her husband Howard doesn't seem to care particularly — until one night she comes home from a party to discover he has packed his things and intends to leave her for good. Panicked, Willie grabs Howard's gun and shoots him dead. With the help of her current paramour, Howard's clever cousin Quincy, the body is disposed of — but unbeknownst to either of them, their problems are only just beginning . . .

A CORNISH VENGEANCE

Rena George

Silas Venning, millionaire owner of a luxury yacht company, is found hanged in a remote Cornish wood. It looks like suicide — but his widow, celebrated artist Laura Anstey, doesn't think so. She enlists Loveday Ross to help prove her suspicions. But there can be no doubts about the killing of Venning's former employee Brian Penrose — not when he's mown down by a hit-and-run driver right in front of Loveday's boyfriend, DI Sam Kitto. Could they be dealing with *two* murders?